Poor Old Ernie

by
Marian R. Bartch
and
Jerry J. Mallett

VANDALIA ROAD • JACKSONVILLE, IL 62650

J
B
c.2

Carlton Press edition published 1983
PERMA-BOUND edition January 1988

Published by PERMA-BOUND, Vandalia Road
            Jacksonville, Illinois 62650
ISBN: 0-8479-9036-2
Printed in the United States of America

For William J. McBride
in appreciation of his personal friendship
and professional support.

PROLOGUE

Well, if you remember anything about me at all, you'll know that the bombshell exploded just two weeks ago today. Yes, that's right, and even though it was two weeks ago I still haven't recovered from the shock! Poor old Ernie—that's me, Ernestine Cecelia Tubb—believed, all too trustingly, that when this year was over that her life would settle down into a normal pattern once again. I really thought that there'd be no more of those embarrassing, humiliating incidents that all happened because of the way our family lived last year. What about the way the Tubb family lived, you ask? Well, let me tell you that in all of your wildest dreams you could never guess what kind of lifestyle we had. The Tubb family lived like no other family lived in all of little old Pleasant Valley. Why did we live so differently—let me tell you—although you probably won't believe it!

It was because my parents, my very own natural Mom and Dad, decided to switch jobs with each other just one year and two weeks ago today. Mom started running the family business, Tubb's Hardware Store, and Dad stayed at home, cooking, cleaning, doing the washing . . . the whole domestic bit! He also claimed to be looking after me and my little sister, Bitsey, but it turned out that I was the one who always got stuck, and I mean stuck, with taking care of the little creep. I'm sure that you can see by now why I call myself "poor old Ernie."

I still wake up in the middle of the night, shuddering over all of those terrible things that happened to me last year because of the big job switch. The nightmare at the Pleasant Valley Community Swimming Pool, my over-starched skirt that gave that horrible loudmouth John Murphy more to tease me about, my futile rescue attempt of Bitsey's cat, Claude, that led to the "trick-or-treat" night disaster, the Thanksgiving turmoil, the confusion at Christmastime, the disgraceful experience at our store, sledding with Bitsey and Dad, the sliding microphones at the school musical, getting locked in the basement closet . . . all rise up to haunt me in the quiet of the night. And, through it all, I hear the echoes of laughter—loudmouth Murphy laughing, laughing, laughing.

The only way I got through that awful year was knowing that when it was over the job switch would be over, and Mom and Dad would be back in their rightful places again. That's what I believed, what I lived for, all through those horrifying months. But that's not the way it happened . . . oh, no, no such luck for poor old Ernie. What happened was this: they decided to go on with this continuation of misery. Mom and Dad took Bitsey and me to dinner to "celebrate" their "good" news that they had decided not to undo the switch, but to go on, probably forever, the way they were. I thought they were joking . . . I just could not bring myself to believe they were serious.

They were, though, they really were, and they expected me to be happy about it. Can you imagine, have you any idea of how I felt at that moment? I just sat there in that lovely restaurant numb with despair when I realized what their decision meant. Then I was cheered up by a thought that I had, a faint glimmer of hope for next year. Next year, and all of the years after, had to be better for me for one very simple reason . . . there was absolutely no way that they could possibly be any worse!

That was the thought that comforted and sustained me, that eased my pain . . . they just couldn't be any worse. I kept believing that right up until yesterday when something else took place that led to . . . but let me begin at the beginning.

Poor Old Ernie

CHAPTER ONE

"Bye, Louise . . . Bye, Mrs. Baldwin . . . thanks again for taking me along," I hollered as their car pulled away. Louise, who is my very dearest best friend, her mom and I had spent the entire day at the Miracle View Shopping Plaza and were we ever tired! Louise and I had tried on dozens and dozens of clothes, but hadn't bought a thing except new swimsuits. We must have stayed later than I realized, because Mom's car was already in the driveway. She usually gets home around six o'clock from the hardware store. "Hm . . . no wonder I'm hungry," I thought.

I started trudging slowly up the sidewalk and was nearly bowled over when the screen door crashed open and Bitsey came flying out to greet me. She was squealing out another one of her crazy-mouthed, mixed-up messages over and over again. I must say here and now that nobody, absolutely nobody, can garble words the way Bitsey can.

"Ernie! Ernie!" she exploded, "we're going on a vaccination!" Now I ask you . . . is she or is she not a dingbat? It was impossible for me to ignore her and her senseless message as I

5

normally would, for she kept dancing and prancing around me, repeating that same stupid sentence again and again in her usual sing-song fashion.

"Bitsy," I explained wearily, mustering up every ounce of patience that a mature sixth-grader could have, "people do not *go* on vaccinations. People *have* vaccinations. People go to a doctor to get vaccinations." I thought that even a little creep like her could understand my super-simple explanation.

Just then Chester, who lives down the street, came "mooing" across our front lawn. Yes, that's what I said—"mooing!" You see, each week Chester decides to be a different animal, and this week was his "cow" week. I simply cannot understand how his second-grade teacher tolerated him this past year. I've said before that Chester is a little light on brain power and now he's given us proof-positive that he's lost his marbles somewhere along the way. It's no surprise to me that he and Bitsey get along so beautifully together.

"Chester," shouted little mis-information, "we're going on a vaccination!"

"Mooo . . . I had mine since before I went to Kindergarten," He replied. "My mommy told me that I was a real brave little boy because I only cried a little bit."

Bitsey looked somewhat puzzled by the cow's comment. Meanwhile, Chester got down on all fours and proceeded to pull up grass with his teeth. He slowly munched away on his fodder, crooning a soft "mooo" between chews.

"Why did you cry when you went on your vaccination?" puzzled Bitsey. I could tell she was beginning to have second thoughts about this "vaccination" thing that had excited her

6

so much in the beginning.

"Mooo," fell from Chester's mouth along with a big clump of grass that he couldn't swallow, "because it hurt when the doctor stuck the needle in my arm."

It was obvious from the look on Bitsey's face that the words of the cow had struck terror in her heart. Tears welled up in her eyes, and she suddenly whirled around and made a mad dash for the front door, screaming all the while as if she were being murdered. I tore myself away from the less-than-fascinating presence of Chester the cow and followed the howling siren into the house.

As I entered the front hall, I saw Mom racing up the stairs with a worried expression on her face. From the wail of the siren I could tell that Bitsey was just ahead of her. Then Dad came rushing in from the kitchen.

"What on earth did you do to your little sister?" he growled.

"Me . . . me . . . I didn't do anything to the little dingbat," I answered defensively. "Why don't you go out and ask the cow on the front lawn?"

But Dad paid no attention, he was too busy scurrying up the steps like a volunteer fireman.

"Well, Ernie, welcome home. We missed having you around the house today," I said to myself. "Did you have a good time shopping with Louise? Did you find anything nice to buy? Aren't you tired and hungry?"

"Why, yes, thank you, to all of your questions," I answered myself, "how considerate of you to ask. It's certainly nice to know that someone around here cares about me."

Just then, I heard a long, mournful moo floating off down

7

the sidewalk as Chester headed for his home.

"Ernie," yelled Dad. "Come up here this minute."

And so Ernestine Cecelia Tubb, obedient family slave, plodded up the stairway to the accompaniment of a loud, loud chorus of wailing, courtesy of her charming little sister.

Mom was on her knees outside the bathroom door.

"Honey," she was talking directly to the doorknob, "please stop crying and unlock this door."

"Now let's have it, Ernestine," thundered Dad. "What went on outside to cause this?"

I could tell that he was really upset because (1) his complexion had changed from normal to red with a tendency to purple, and (2) he referred to me by my full name instead of Ernie. I felt like I was being cross-examined by the district attorney. I began my defense by pleading ignorance.

"All I know is that Bitsey told Chester (I decided to leave out the cow routine) and me something about a vaccination and so Chester told her that it hurt when he got one before he started school . . . *and I didn't do or say anything!*"

A loud piercing shriek came from the other side of the door.

"And I don't wanna go on any vaccination!"

Mom turned around, looked at Dad, and though they both tried not to, broke into laughter. Their laughter was punctuated by heartbroken crying interrupted only by screams of "NO VACCINATION!"

Even I was beginning to feel sorry for her, but as it turned out, my sympathy was sadly misplaced. I should have been feeling sorry for poor old Ernie, not Bitsey.

"Bitsey . . . oh, Bitsey, honey . . . listen to me," called Mom.

"You don't have to have the shot, honey."

"That's right, Bitsey," reinforced Dad, "we're going on a *vacation,* not a *vaccination.* Chester just got you all mixed up."

"Chester got *her* all mixed up" I began, "good grief, it was the bird-brain who got . . . ." Glares from both of my parents stopped me in mid-sentence. "Well, now," I thought, "isn't that just like them. I try to explain what *really* happened, and they get mad at ME! Bitsey never gets the worst of it, oh, no, never Bitsey. Dear, sweet, cute, clever little Bitsey . . . ." I turned away and went into my bedroom, thinking it would be nice if she never came out of the bathroom. I did leave my door open a crack, though, to see how long she would stay there. Mom and Dad both kept coaxing her to unlock the door. I was still fuming over the injustice of it all while changing out of my clothes, when all of a sudden it hit me. I raced out into the hall and yelled loudly, "A VACATION! Oh . . . wow . . . a vacation. Where . . . where are we going? When are we going?"

Dad looked at me and a big grin slowly spread over his face.

"Yes, Ernie, you got it . . . a vacation. Your Mom has done such a great job of running the store this past year that we decided the Tubb family could take a really nice vacation this summer."

Mom was too busy talking to the little creep to hear Dad's compliment.

"Where are we going? When? How long can we stay?"

"Hold on," laughed Dad. "We've rented a cottage at Kickapoo Lake for a week and we leave Tuesday."

"Kickapoo Lake! Oh, Dad, that's great. That's just great."

Kickapoo Lake was just about the most popular resort area

near Pleasant Valley. The kids at school all talked about it since most of them have been there with their families. It was a great place to camp on weekends. I myself had been there once with Louise's family and had a super time.

I was rudely jolted from my thoughts about Kickapoo Lake and the fun I could have there by an unusually loud shriek followed by "I can't, can't, can't!"

"Of course you can, honey," soothed Mom. "All you have to do is to push that little button under the doorknob."

We could hear some fumbling noises on the other side of the door, then silence. Mom tried the door, but it wouldn't open.

"Bitsey," she pleaded, "Please try again.'

There were more fumbling noises, more silence. Then in a quietly quavering voice our little locksmith whimpered, "It won't move . . . I can't do it. Mommy, I want out . . . get me out . . . NOW!" The quavering voice gathered volume at the end of her sentence.

"Now, now, Bitsey, don't worry," comforted Mom. "Daddy will get you out."

Dad got organized.

"Right, Bitsey, I'll have you out in no time. Ernie, run down to the basement and bring up my screwdrivers."

I wanted to ask him if his leg was broken, but thought better of it just in time. Instead, I, Ernie the workhorse, meekly descended to the basement while Mom and Dad made reassuring noises to Bitsey trying to keep her in a semi-calm state. I made the return trip quickly with several different sized screwdrivers and Dad went to work trying to pry open the lock.

Unfortunately, all of Dad's efforts proved futile, and the lock stayed locked, the door stayed closed, and the tearful Bitsey stayed inside in a state bordering on panic. All of this turned out to be a very unfortunate state of affairs for me because of what followed.

Dad finally gave up, saying, "We'll have to approach it from another direction. The only thing left to do is to get the ladder and crawl in through the window from the outside."

Now you might be wondering, as I was, just who could be expected to do this highly dangerous job of crawling into an upstairs window from a ladder. And you probably won't be surprised, as I wasn't, to find out just who that someone turned out to be.

Dad said in that no-nonsense tone of voice I knew so well, "Come on Ernie." There, wouldn't you know! Now poor old *Ernie* had to risk her life doing tricky acrobatics to rescue her incompetent little dingbat of a sister.

"Vacation, hah!" I thought. "I'll be lucky if I live to enjoy it."

Dad propped the ladder under the bathroom window and told me, "Now, Ernie, I want you to be very careful. I'll hold the ladder steady so it won't wobble. When you reach the window, simply unlatch the screen and toss it down to me. Then all you have to do is to crawl in through the window."

I must have looked as nervous as I felt, for he added, "I'd do it myself, honey, but the window is so small I don't think I could get through it."

Up the ladder climbed Ernie the brave. All I could think of was my last rescue attempt when Claude was stranded on the garage roof and what a hopeless disaster it was. I felt like a prisoner going to her doom. Thank goodness that it was Dad who was holding the ladder for me instead of Chester the cow like before.

"Be careful," cautioned Dad, as I neared the top of the ladder and reached for the screen latch. It was pretty rusty, so I had to really work with it before it broke loose. As I pulled the screen out of the window frame I heard a long, low moo. Yes, of course, Chester the cow was returning to our pasture.

"Moooo . . ." he moaned as he rounded the side of our house. "Moo . . . watcha doing, Ernie?" he asked as I tossed the screen down to Dad.

"That's good," encouraged Dad, ignoring the cow. "Now be very careful crawling through the window. There may be some splinters."

"Mooo . . . watcha crawling through the window for?"

"Oh, good grief, Chester," I hollered down at him, "because I feel like it."

"Mooo . . ." came his reply, "can I crawl through it too?"

"Chester," Dad broke in, "Please don't bother Ernie now. Bitsey has locked herself in the bathroom and Ernie is going through the window to unlock the door."

"Mooo . . . I wanna watch Ernie."

"Okay," said Dad. "Just don't bother her."

"Oh, great," I thought, "just what I need, an audience." It was a wonder that the photographer from the Pleasant Valley Evening Gazette hadn't shown up like he did when I got locked in the basement.

For the first time I looked into the bathroom window and . . . are you ready for what I saw? Well, there sat Bitsey in the place of honor looking right back at me with a big smile on her tear-stained face.

"Hi, Ernie," was her simple greeting followed by an even simpler question. "Did you bring Claudie with you?"

I couldn't be bothered to answer her, I just shot her a glare and started crawling through the window. Dad was right, he would have had trouble getting through that window because I was having great difficulty. My head and shoulder squeezed through without too much trouble, but that was the easy part. From that point on, I had to struggle to get in without the support of the ladder since I was hanging over the window ledge like a broken teeter-totter. I was looking around for something inside to grab hold of to pull myself in, when Bitsey came up with another of her simple questions.

"Are you mad at me, Ernie?"

"Why, no, of course not," I replied in my nicey-nicey tone of voice. "Why on earth should I be mad? I just love to risk my life this way."

"I've got something to tell you, Ernie," said the stoolsitter.

"For heaven's sake, Bitsey," I grumbled, "I'm in no mood for conversation now. Just sit there and don't say another word or you'll be sorry."

"But Ernie . . ." she went on.

"No, Bitsey, not another word!" I commanded.

"Mooo . . ." commented the cow. "Are you stuck?"

I heard Dad remind Chester not to bother me as I made a grab for the sink. Unfortunately I couldn't reach it, but found that I could just reach the towel rack. I got a good, strong grip on it with my left hand, and began pulling my body through the window.

"Be careful, Ernie," Mom called from behind the door.

She had no sooner said this when a frightening thing happened. The towel rack simply pulled right out of the wall! This, of course, threw me off-balance and I had to wave my arms and legs wildly to keep from crashing to my death at the bottom of the ladder next to my Dad and the cow.

Now, are you ready for what poor old Ernie had to cope with next? Well, let me tell you that Ernestine Cecelia Tubb wasn't ready for anything of the sort. My crazy gyrations had jiggled the window so much that it slowly slid down just like a guillotine, coming to rest firmly on my back. So there I was— just hanging there—unable to move in or out, up or down, due to the vise-like death-grip of the window. As I hung there, calling for help, wondering how to solve this unbelievable predicament, the little wonder, who had been taking all of this very quietly, got off her throne, walked to the door, and—can you believe this?—turned the knob and opened the door!

Mom gasped and ran in. She grabbed me by the arms while Dad, who must have broken all speed records climbing the ladder, pushed the window open. With Dad pushing and Mom pulling, I managed to slide through the window, landing in a heap on the bathroom floor.

"Ernie, Ernie," called Mom. "Are you alright?"

"Mom," I breathed, staring at the little creep in wonderment. "Mom, she . . . she unlocked the door. I mean, she did it all by herself. I mean . . . Bitsey could do it all the time!"

"Are you hurt, Ernie?" asked Dad from outside.

"She did it all by herself. She opened the door and walked right out." I could hardly believe what I had seen.

14

"That's what I had to tell you, Ernie," said Bitsey, "but you said...."

"Never mind, Bitsey, don't bother Ernie now," commanded Mom, leading her younger daughter away.

And then, then the little demon demonstrated what had to be the tops in ungratefulness by skipping down the hall whining, "Ernie didn't bring Claudie."

I couldn't believe it. I just simply could not believe it. Here I had almost died trying to help her highness when she didn't need any help in the first place, and all she has to say is, "Ernie didn't bring Claudie."

What an ordeal ... but at least it was over and I had our vacation to look forward to. The Tubbs would soon be leaving Pleasant Valley, which has yet to prove very "pleasant" for yours truly, to spend a marvelous week at Kickapoo Lake. One long, relaxing, trouble-free week away from Pleasant Valley, away from all of Ernestine Cecelia Tubb's cares and worries!

Oh, brother ... if I had any inkling then of what I would be going through at Kickapoo Lake, I would have turned around and leaped right out of that bathroom window!

CHAPTER TWO

As a result of the great "bathroom-window disaster," we adults of the Tubb family now referred to our upcoming vacation as our "trip-to-the-lake," for no one, especially me, wanted to risk setting off any more Bitsey-generated dumbness by confusion. Anyway, the days following this unforgettable incident were spent in getting together things we'd need to take with us. For Bitsey, that meant only one thing, her Claudie. I was sorting through my shorts, deciding which ones to take when all of a sudden I was hit with another of my "Ernie specials." These are super-fantastic ideas that I get every now and then, but this was really a super-super-fantastic one that topped every other one I'd ever had. I went dashing down the steps at full speed.

"Dad . . . Dad," I yelled.

"Here . . . here," he answered from the kitchen.

"Oh, hi, Mom," I panted, "I didn't know you were home already."

"Well, we weren't very busy at the store, so Joe's closing up for me. I thought I was needed more here at home. There's

16

a lot to do if we're ever going to get away on our va . . . trip-to-the lake in three days."

Dad turned from the sink where he was working on a salad and said, "I'm delighted you're home early, but you don't have to worry about packing. I have everything almost ready to go right now."

Then he remembered his forgotten girl.

"What do you want, Ernie?"

"Oh, Mom, Dad," I looked from one to the other. "I've just had the most marvelous idea! Oh please say yes."

"Well," began Dad, "we might say yes if we knew. . . ."

"Louise, it's Louise . . . couldn't she go with us? It'd be wonderful having her along. Oh, say yes. PULEEZE say yes!" I begged.

Mom and Dad looked at each other and I knew instantly from the smiles on both of their faces that the answer *would* be yes.

"Honey," said Mom, "the truth is that your dad and I had already talked about it and think it is a great idea. We were going to mention it at dinner tonight."

"Oh . . . wow . . . that's neat!" I exploded.

"Now, wait a minute, Ernie," Dad broke in, "before you get too excited. You and Louise will have to share the hide-a-bed. Mr. Bumbee, the owner of the cottage, said that it folds out to make a double bed."

"Oh, that's okay, Louise and I won't mind a bit. Can I call her right now and ask her?"

"Be my guest," said Dad.

Well, let me tell you I broke my own record dialing Louise's

17

number. She was as excited as I was at the prospect of spending a whole, entire week together at Kickapoo Lake. We made our plans within minutes, and I rushed back to the kitchen to share the good news.

"She can go . . . she can go with us," I bubbled.

"That's great, Ernie," commented Dad. Mom must have gone upstairs to change clothes while I was on the phone since she wasn't in the kitchen any longer.

"Ernie," Dad went on, "I need some more lettuce for the salad. Fill this bowl with it, will you please? And check on Bitsey while you're out there."

I was so happy about Louise going along, I didn't even mind having to do the chores again. As I went out the back door, I heard Bitsey talking to her precious Claude. I just stopped short and looked at the two of them for a minute to make sure that I really saw what I thought I was seeing. Bitsey was a wonder to behold, standing in her Mickey Mouse swimming pool in all of three inches of water. You would be sure, looking at her, though, that she was preparing to swim the Atlantic Ocean. In additional to her swimsuit, she was wearing her Flipper swim fins, Goofy water-goggles, that were on upside-down, her snorkel mask draped around her neck, and her Lucky-Ducky swim ring. Claude was sitting about two feet away from her, keeping a cautious distance. She was obviously giving swimming instructions to Claude who didn't seem to be able to take his eyes off her. He probably thought that he had just witnessed the first landing of a Martian.

"See, Claudie . . . this is how you swim. You have to learn so you can swim with me at the Kipoowee Lake."

18

"Bitsey, in the first place we are going to Kickapoo Lake . . . *not* Kipoowee Lake! As far as I know there is no such place as Kipoowee Lake except in your head. For once could you please get the right name for something. And," I went on, "Claudie is not going to swim with you, everyone knows that cats cannot swim."

"Claudie knows how to swim, he's really going to have fun swimming with me at Kipoowee Lake," was the stubborn reply of mixed-up mouth.

"I give up! I don't know why I even try." I turned away in disgust and headed for the garden. I was busy picking lettuce when I heard Chester the Chicken come clucking into our yard. Oh, yes, I should explain that Chester is no longer a cow. Two days ago he went to bed mooing and woke up the next morning clucking.

"Cluck, cluck, cluck . . . hi, Bitsey. Hi, Claude. Cluck, cluck, cluck . . . hi, Ernie," he said as he bobbed and pecked his way across our backyard. He sat down beside the Mickey Mouse pool next to Claude. Claude turned his back to him. Poultry have rather an unnerving effect on Claude ever since our unfortunate incident at Turkle's Turkey Farm last year.

"Cluck, cluck . . . hi, Chester," answered Bitsey, wanting to speak Chickenese too. Claude turned his head around to glare at Chester, apparently upset at having his swimming lesson interrupted. I simply continued picking lettuce and tried to ignore the two chickens. Little did I know that this would soon be impossible, thanks to Tinkerbell. Yes, Tinkerbell, Chester's dog. The two of them are usually inseparable. Now when you think of a dog named Tinkerbell you probably imagine a small, lovely little dog, good-natured, dainty, and intelligent, as I did before I laid eyes on Chester's pet. Where Chester ever even heard that name let alone thought it fit for such a huge, ugly dumb dog is beyond me. Tinkerbell looks like a cross between a sheepdog and a giant jackrabbit, and, as to her intelligence, I'd say it was about on the same level as Chester's. Well, maybe a little above but she is friendly, I will have to say that for her . . . if only she drooled a little less.

"Cluck, cluck . . . whatcha doin' . . . cluck, cluck," asked the chicken.

"Cluck, cluck . . . showing Claudie how to swim," answered the chicken-mermaid.

"Cluck, cluck . . whatcha doing, Ernie?" was chicken-brain's next brilliant question.

"Good grief, Chester, what does it look like I'm doing?"

"Cluck, cluck . . . betcha you're looking for worms."

"I am not, you big, dumb cluck!" I had completely lost patience with Chester the chicken.

Then a strange sight accompanied by an equally strange noise on the other side of our big wooden back fence caught my attention. What I could see over the top of the fence looked exactly like a man or woman wearing a bearskin hat, but the hat kept bobbing up and down and making the oddest noises, almost like a baby crying. I took a closer look and discovered it was man's, I mean chicken's, best friend. Yes, it was Tinkerbell, jumping up and down to see Chester, crying to be helped over the fence so she could be with her beloved master. It was probably just a coincidence that Tinkerbell never noticed that she was standing right next to the open gate.

"Chester," I called, "go help Tinkerbell the genius-dog into the yard."

That was a big mistake on my part. I should have just paid no attention to that clumsy animal, for the minute that Chester dragged her into our yard, she caused trouble. Tinkerbell and Claude had never met before, and neither waited for polite introductions. Tinkerbell let out a combination growl and howl and made a mad, uncoordinated dash in Claude's direction. But Claude hadn't stayed there waiting to properly greet his guest. I don't believe I've ever seen him move so fast. His tail and whiskers went straight up and he practically flew up the nearest tree where he sat yowling and hissing.

Well, what happened next can best be described as indescribable chaos. Bitsey began screaming as if her beloved Claudie was in mortal danger, with intermittent clucks by Chester in the background.

"Claudie, Claudie, come (cluck) here."

Tinkerbell continued her howling and growling while jumping up and down around the tree. Claude, forgetting his duties as a host, continued yowling and hissing, and began taking swipes at Tinkerbell's nose with his paw.

Chester then forgot that he was a chicken and began jumping around the foot of the tree trying to catch Tinkerbell while yelling at her.

"Heel, Tinkerbell, heel, heel," Chester shouted.

"Ernie, Ernie, help Claudie," Bitsey shouted.

I tried to yell over all the noise, "Chester, will you please shut that dumb dog up!"

"Ernie, Ernie," shrieked our little swim queen as she pointed up into the tree. I looked up just in time to see Claude, the brave defender of home and self, make a mightly lunge at Tinkerbell's head with his outstretched paw—oh, he was a ferocious sight to see! Tinkerbell's eyes took on a wild look as she ducked out of the way. Poor Claude missed Tinkerbell, lost his balance and began to fall from the tree. He made a mighty effort to change direction in mid-air so that he could reach the safety of the garage roof. His effort was marvelous, the result was not—he missed completely. His death-defying leap took him from the tree branch to—no, not the roof of the garage, but to—are you ready for this one—the head of Tinkerbell the Terrible. This so stunned everyone that there was a deathly silence for approximately one second—then the real circus began. Tinkerbell ran in a circle, howling all the while, with Claude perched atop her head. Claude, however, was not facing forwards. Being Claude he had landed backwards but he dug his claws in for dear life around Tinkerbell's neck. Tinkerbell could only see out of one eye at a time, for Claude kept switching his tail back and forth, first covering one eye, then the other. Bitsey screamed like *she* was being murdered now, and Chester joined in, running after his dog while yelling at Claude, "Get off, get off my Tinkerbell!" Neither animal paid any attention.

Now what happened next should go into Ripley's *Believe It or Not* book, for as I, Ernestine Cecelia Tubb, attempted to restore some semblance of order in this mad group, Tinkerbell the tornado headed directly for me. There was only one thing I could do to avoid being run down by the Tank and I did it, thinking quickly, as always. I made a fast step back and to the left and she missed me completely. But before I had time to congratulate myself on my resourcefulness, a terrible thing happened. I tripped over the edge of the Mickey Mouse pool and fell backwards into it. At the very same time, Claude either leaped or was thrown from the wild bronco's back and came to rest on my very soggy lap. Now, minus his tormentor, and with full sight once again, Tinkerbell made a mad rush to escape from the yard and sailed over the fence with a mighty bound—and she *almost* cleared it—almost. Chester ran after her, helped her through the gate and a quietness descended over the Tubb yard.

Bitsey grabbed Claude away from me and proceeded to lavish love, care and sympathy on him.

"Poor Claudie," she crooned, "poooor Claudie. Bad old Ernie let the terrible dog chase you. Poor Claudie."

Claude looked up at me and I swear there was a smirk on his face.

I was limp. I couldn't even move or do anything but just sit there, wet from head to toe, in the little mermaid's Mickey Mouse pool.

Hoots of laughter, hollers of mirth, exploded from inside the kitchen. Through the window, I could see Dad, holding his sides and shaking. Sometimes my dad shows a very odd sense of humor. I could not see anything at all to laugh at. Nothing funny was going on.

From far off down the street I heard, "Cluck, cluck, cluck, cluck, cluck, cluck." Chester, of course, apparently making up for missed clucks!

"You've got to be strong, Ernie, strong," I said to myself.

"Hang in there, no matter what happens. Only three more days . . . three more days to live through until Kickapoo Lake." I just hoped I'd make it.

CHAPTER THREE

"Help, Chester, save me. Help me, Chester!" I screamed as I ran down our sidewalk.

"Help . . . Chester! There's a giant chicken after me!"

I was trying to run, but no matter how hard I tried, I couldn't make my legs go fast. They felt like they were made of lead. The chicken was gaining on me, and it had a frightening grin on its beak.

"I knew that if I could only get to Chester's house, I'd be safe there—he knew all about chickens.

"Help me!" I yelled again.

"Ernie . . . Ernie . . . what's the matter?" It was Louise's voice.

"It's the chicken . . . he's almost got me. Look out, Louise, he'll be after you, too!" I warned her.

"Ernie . . . wake up!" said Louise, shaking my shoulder. "You're okay, you're just having a bad dream."

I sat up in bed and rubbed my eyes. There was no giant chicken, just Louise and me in my room. I began to feel terribly silly.

"Oh, Louise, it *was* a dream, wasn't it. But is was the most awful dream—and so real. All about a giant chicken and Chester."

My explanation was punctuated by a loud crash in the distance, followed by a long, low rumble. The loudness of the noise, combined with the emotional state I was in from the nightmare, almost catapulted me out of bed. Louise did get up and grope her way to the window.

"Oh, no," she cried. "It's awfully dark outside. It sure looks like we're going to have a storm."

"Oh, rats," I said, "here it is, the first day of our vacation and it's going to rain. I feel like pulling the covers up over my head and staying in bed, but I might go back to sleep and the chicken *would* get me."

Since we were leaving very early in the morning for our cottage at Kickapoo Lake, Louise had stayed overnight at our house. She had brought her suitcase and two brown paper bags full of things to take along on our week's vacation. Everything the Tubbs were taking was all packed and ready to go except for a few things that needed to be kept in the refrigerator until the last minute.

Even though it was very early, there was no peace and quiet in the house. From down the hall floated strains of a tune I knew well, "The Farmer in the Dell." Yes, the tune was familiar, but the lyrics were strictly brand-new Bitsey originals.

> Kipoowee here we come,
> Kipoowee here we come,
> Hi Ho Kipoowee Lake,
> Kipoowee here we come.

Of course, being Bitsey, she had to sing it over and over and over again, each chorus gaining volume over the last. Louise laughed and thought it was cute.

"Wouldn't you think," I commented, "wouldn't you think that just once, just once, that old crazy-mouth could get at least one name straight?"

"Oh, she's so funny," said Louise.

"Geez, Louise," I answered, "you wouldn't think so if you had to live with her craziness day in and day out like I do. Well, at least we don't have to go through the ordeal of waking her up. *That* can be a major undertaking."

"Bahroom!" came another long roll of thunder.

"Gee," said Louise, "it sounds like it's getting closer."

"Hey girls," Dad hollered from downstairs, "get a move on. We want to be in the car before it begins to rain."

Well, that sure made us move. We rushed down the hall to the bathroom to wash up. We were brushing our teeth when you might know, the songbird waddled in, still in her nightgown.

"Bitsey gotta go tinkle," trilled the little twerp.

"You'th haffa way," I said with my mouth full of toothpaste.

She stamped her foot, "No, Bitsey gotta go tinkle *now!*" Then she began to cross her legs and hop around.

"Thorry," I said through my toothpaste to Louise and pointed to the hallway. Bitsey prefers to be alone in the bathroom. We both must have looked like mad dogs frothing at the mouths as we walked into the hall. Bitsey closed the door while repeating in her well-known sing-song fashion, "Tinkly, tinkle Bitsey gotta go ... tinkle, tinkly, Bitsey gotta go!" Then all

27

was quiet. Minutes went by and no sound from the little princess. Louise and I stood in the hall with our toothpaste drying around our mouths.

"Ould you urry up?" I said, through the dribble of toothpaste running down my chin.

And then Bitsey began her dumb song again, showing absolutely no concern for time, her sister, or her sister's friend. While I fumed, she sang:

> Kipoowee here we come,
> Kipoowee here we come,
> Hi Ho Kipoowee Lake,
> Kipoowee here we come.

"I think I'm going to strangle her," I said to myself.

Then when her highness was good and ready, she opened the door (forgetting to flush, of course) and skipped down the hall right in front of us, to her bedroom.

"Louise, Ernie," she called, "you'd better hurry, you'll make us late."

"Now I know I'm going to strangle her," I repeated to myself. Then she resumed singing her dippy little song, but with a smashing new twist.

> Kipoowee here we come,
> Kipoowee here we come,
> Kipoowee Lake, Kipoowee Lake,
> Dumb—Dumb—Dumb!

Well, my day had certainly started in the typical way, but I wasn't really upset because I knew it was going to change from mediocre to marvelous.

We just had time for a quick breakfast and the last minute

packing before the storm hit. We were in the car pulling out of the driveway when "BAHROOM!" The thunder was so loud that it could have been in the car with us. Bitsey, who was sitting between Louise and me in the back seat, was scared out of her wits, what she had of them. She jerked and grabbed hold of my arm like the world was coming to an end. Claude, who had been lounging on Bitsey's lap, leaped at least a foot, then shot straight under the front seat. All we saw of him after that for the rest of the trip was an occasional glimpse of his scraggly tail twitching every now and then.

With that last mighty clap of thunder, came the rain. And when the skies opened, so did our little nightingale's mouth, in a rendition of another one of her mixed-up melodies.

> Rain, rain, go away,
> Humpelty Dumpelty had a great fall,
> And Claudie wants to play.

I stood the songs as long as I could—about one minute—then blurted out, "Bitsey, will you please stop singing those . . ."

Mom quickly turned her head and gave me a glare, so I restrained myself from finishing my sentence which would have been ". . . those dumb, dim-witted songs!"

"I know what we can do," said Louise, "Let's play a game."

"Oh, goody," exclaimed Bitsey. "I just love games."

"That would be nice," approved Mom.

"Let's play hopscotch," bubbled the little game expert.

"Hotscotch!" I repeated in disbelief. "Hopscotch! How could we play hopscotch in the car?"

"I know a good game to play in the car," said Louise. "It's called, 'I went to the store.' First, one person says, 'I went to

29

the store and bought' something. Ernie might say, 'I went to the store and bought a bicycle.' The I would have to repeat what she said and add something else. I might say, ' went to the store and bought a bicycle and a dress.' The the next person would have to remember those two things and add a third. Do you understand, Bitsey?"

"Bicycle and a dress!!! I won!" yelled Bitsey at the top of her lungs. It was a wonder Dad didn't go right off of the road.

"Good grief," I muttered.

"No, Bitsey, I was just explaining how to play," corrected Louise.

"Why don't you girls just begin and I'll help Bitsey get started," said Mom, giving Louise a wink.

"Okay," said Louise. "Ernie, you begin."

"I went to the store and bought a can of tomatoes."

"I went to the store," continued Louise, " and bought a can of tomatoes and a loaf of wheat bread. Okay, Bitsey . . . now it's your turn."

"Oh, brother," I thought to myself. "This'll be good."

"First you say 'I went to the store,'" coached Mom.

"I went to the store . . ." Bitsey stopped.

"Now, can you remember what Ernie and Louise bought?" asked Mom.

Bitsey nodden a vigorous yes.

"Well then, tell us!" I blurted out.

With a smile of confidence on her face, she hollered, "A can of Pete's bread and a bamatoe."

"I give up," I groaned.

"That's not quite right, honey," said Mom, giving me a look.

She whispered in Bitsey's ear. Bitsey's eyes lit up and then she said, "A can of bamatoes and pete's bread."

"That's close enough," said Louise, trying to hide her smile. "Now you get to choose something to buy at the store."

"I wanna buy . . ." after a long pause during which you could almost see the thoughts whirling around in Bitsey's head, she blurted out, "a great big wooly worm!" I groaned to myself to avoid getting another one of those looks from Mom.

"I went to the store," I said, continuing the game, "and bought a can of TOMATOES, and a loaf of WHOLE WHEAT bread, and a DUMB big, wooly worm, *and* a package of spaghetti."

Louise was next and she began, "I went to the . . ."

"Hold on, everybody," shouted Dad as he braked the car and steered to the side of the highway.

"What's the matter?" asked Mom and I together.

"Bitsey can't see Kipoowee Lake yet," chimed in the great traveler.

Dad disgustedly replied, "I'm afraid we've got a flat tire."

"Oh, no," cried Mom.

"Who's a fat liar?" asked the little know-nothing.

Even Mom gave up on trying to explain this time. Dad got out of the car to take a look. Within a second, he stuck his head in the window and said, "Yep, it's the back left tire. I'll have to change it."

"Oh, honey," sympathized Mom, "that's too bad."

"Well, look on the bright side . . . at least the rain has slowed down to a drizzle, " answered Dad as he headed for the tools in the trunk.

He had it changed within thirty minutes, thirty *long*

minutes for those of us in that back seat with Bitsey the Bouncer.

"Well, now," he said, getting back in the car, "that wasn't too bad, was it?"

"Oh, Mr. Tubb," said Louise, "your shirt is all wet!"

"And look at your shoes," cried Mom, "They're caked with mud."

"Oh, yeah," said Dad, looking down at his feet. "I'm afraid I chose a very soft shoulder to pull off on. Oh, well, it's over now and I can clean off my shoes when we get to our cottage at Kickapoo."

That was all the cue Bitsey needed to set off on her dumb song again.

> Kipoowee here we come,
> Kipoowee here we come,
> Hi Ho the stereo,
> Kipoowee here we come.

Dad started the car and shifted into drive as the songbird happily trilled away. He gave the car some gas, but nothing happened. It didn't even move an inch. He tried again, but still nothing.

"Bitsey, honey," said Mom, "please stop singing. Dad's having trouble with the car."

"Thank goodness for small favors," I thought to myself.

Dad put the car in reverse and gunned it. It jerked, but didn't move very much. Forward and back, forward and back . . . the more Dad tried to move the car, the lower it sunk on the right side. Finally, he heaved a great sigh, and said, "I guess we're going to have to give it a push."

Now you might ask just what Dad meant when he said *we're*

going to have to give it a push. I was especially intrigued by his use of the word "we're." Surely, you might say, he can't expect a certain young lady and the young lady's friend to tromp through the mud in the rain in order to *push*. Well, think again!

Naturally the little twerp didn't have to help. She was getting terribly excited by this turn of events and hollered, "Bitsey help, too," as we were getting out of the car.

"Bitsey, you can crawl over the front seat and help me," said Mom as she slid over to the driver's side.

"Boy, some help," I thought.

Dad positioned himself on the right side of the car where the wheel had sunk into the mud. I braced myself behind the other wheel, and Louise was between the two of us.

"When I count to three," he said, loudly enough for Mom to hear, "give the car some gas and we'll push. Okay . . . one, two, three."

Well, we pushed and pushed, but nothing much happened. I mean, the car didn't budge.

"Honey," hollered Dad, all out of breath, "give it more gas next time and see if that makes a difference. Here we go again . . . one." On the count of one, Ernestine Cecelia Tubb should have prepared herself for impending disaster.

"Two."

On the count of two, Ernestine Cecelia Tubb should have hopped back into the safety of the car.

"Three!"

On the count of three, Ernestine Cecelia Tubb should have crawled under the front seat next to Claude.

But no . . . unsuspecting, willing-to-do-her-share-and-more

33

Ernie did not do any of the above. Instead, on the count of three, she became a living mud puddle! For on the count of three, Mom really gunned the car which resulted in (1) the car pulling loose from the mud, (2) the spinning of the left wheel, where poor old Ernie stood so steadfastly pushing, at a rapid speed, causing (3) a tremendous spray of mud that ended up as a head-to-toe coating on Ernestine Cecelia Tubb!

I heard Louise's voice, but it seemed to be coming from a great distance.

"Oh, Ernie . . . oh, Ernie," she kept repeating.

I remember thinking, "It's strange how everything sounds so different through five inches of mud,"

The mud had plastered my eyes and mouth shut, and as I stood there speechless and unseeing, I could fell it begin to ooze down my back. In the next instant, someone took hold of my hand while someone else wiped off my face. Then I was led up to where the car now waited. Mom had the trunk open already and was hurriedly searching through the suitcases. She found some large towels and did her best to wipe away as much as possible.

"Oh, dear. Oh, honey . . . Ernie," she moaned, "are you alright?"

"Why I'm just peachy-keen!" I thought to myself. "How else could I be now that I've been transformed into a soggy mud-pie." But out loud, I said, "I guess so."

'Oh, Ernie," continued Mom, "we'll clean you off as best we can, then you can change and wash up at the cottage . . . how much farther to the lake?" she turned to Dad.

"I'd say about five miles," returned Dad as we all got back

into our mud-splattered heap. "Won't be long at all, Ernie."

"Oh, sure . . . not long at all!" I screamed to myself as I sat on the back seat huddled in towels. Well maybe not for everybody else, but it could prove to be an eternity for someone whose mudpack was beginning to crust.

"Well, Ernestine," I said to myself, "here you are on the threshold of your long-awaited vacation. The fun is just beginning!"

CHAPTER FOUR

"Kipoowee, Kipoowee, Kipoowee!" shrieked Bitsey as the car wound around a long, lazy curve in the road giving us our first glimpse of the lake. The closer we got to the lake, the more excited we all became. Even the human mudpie couldn't help but be more than a little thrilled with the sight of Kickapoo Lake. The rain had finally given way to sunshine, which made the lake glisten and sparkle—it was dazzling. Just looking at it made everyone in the car feel good. Dad turned onto a side road with a sign telling us that it was Waterfront Drive.

"Here we are," said Dad. "Now everyone look for our cottage."

"What does it look like?" asked Mom.

"I don't know," answered Dad, "but the address is 9072 Waterfront Drive. It's on this side of the lake and not too far from the public beach."

"Oh, isn't that great!" exclaimed Louise. "We can just *walk* down to the beach. Oh, I just can't wait."

Dad began slowing down as we all helped him look for our cottage—all except you-know-who. She was too busy bounc-

36

ing up and down to the beat for her Kipoowee song.

"I see the public beach," hollered Mom, as excited as the rest of us.

"Good," responded Dad, "then the cottage can't be much farther."

"Do you see that?" I asked Louise. "*Three* diving boards."

"What's that over there?" asked Mom, pointing to a large structure.

"Oh . . . wow!" breathed Louise. "That has to be the new Water Whip. Some of the kids at school were talking about one being built out here—but I didn't think it would be so high."

About a dozen kids were in various stages of descent on this ride and it looked like great fun. It was a giant slide that twisted and turned as it came down. Water was constantly rushing down it along with kids riding on mats. There was a small pool at the bottom that the riders splashed into.

"Boy," I said, "I can hardly wait to try that . . . it sure looks like a lot of fun."

Little did I know then that before this vacation was over I would have reason to *hate* this Water Whip.

Bitsey must have really been enthralled with this giant water slide because she had stopped her singing/bouncing routine and simply stared out the window at all of the action.

Just then, Mom told Dad, "Slow down, Pete, I think I see our cottage. Yes, that's it, the yellow one. Oh, isn't it cute! That's just what I had hoped it would be."

"Yeah, and it really is close to the beach," enthused Louise.

With all the excitement, I had momentarily forgotten about my dilemma, but just then Claude peeked out from under the front seat, glanced in my direction, turned away, glanced at me again, and began to hiss. The poor cat probably thought that the car had been invaded by a mysterious mud monster.

Mom must have noticed, for she reached over to pat my muddy paw saying sympathetically, "Don't worry, honey, you can take a shower soon. We'll be in the cottage in a minute."

Dad pulled into the driveway, stopped the car, turned around in his seat, and said proudly, 'And now our vacation offically begins, an entire week of fun and relaxation, an entire week of swimming and boating, an entire week of fishing and sunning, an . . ."

"An entire week of sitting in the car," Mom broke, in, "unless you stop making a speech."

We all cracked up at this, even Dad.

"Honey, you unlock the cottage while the rest of us unload the car," directed Dad to Mom.

We all began to transfer our cargo to the cottage—all except Bitsey, that is. She spent her time trying to convince Claude that it was alright for him to come out from under the front seat. At least that kept both of the nuisances out of our way.

"Where should I put this, Mom?"

"Over next to the sink, Ernie." Then she added, "Let the others get the rest, you go take your shower. Leave those clothes in the bathroom. They're going to have to be scrubbed several times to get them clean."

"So will poor old Ernie," I thought. Surprisingly enough, though, after five minutes under the warm shower I felt like my old self again.

"Hey, Ernie, you sure look a lot better," grinned Louise as

I came out of the bathroom.

"Thanks, I sure feel a lot better . . . ready to tackle that Water Whip anytime."

"Well, this is the last of it," groaned Dad as he struggled to get one suitcase and two boxes through the cottage door. He shot a glance in my direction, grinned at me and said, "You look better than ever, Ernie. Guess it's true that mudpacks are good for your complexion!"

The rest of us groaned. We just have to tolerate his corny remarks. I was saved from trying to think of a proper reply by the appearance of Bitsey stumbling in carrying a bored-looking Claude.

"Claudie's ready to go swimming!" insisted the little twerp in that piercing voice of her. I had a sudden flashback of holding a terrified Claude in my lap in the Mickey Mouse pool and a shiver ran up my spine.

"Oh, sure," I said, "I'm sure that Claude is just dying to go for a swim."

"Claudie wanna go swimming," was her one-track thought reply. As usual, my clever sarcasm went right over her head.

"Girls," broke in Mom, "help me straighten out this mess and then you can walk down to the beach for a swim."

"Sounds great to me," said Louise.

We went into high gear with the promise of our first swim that close to becoming true. Before we knew it, Mom was saying that she could handle the rest, so please take Bitsey and be off to the lake for a nice swim.

"Bitsey? We have to take Bitsey?" I stared at Mom in disbelief.

"Bitsey ready," said the nuisance, struggling to get into her swim ring.

"Mom," I moaned, "do we have to?"

"No," she answered slyly, "you can stay here and help me with more unpacking."

"Oh, we'll be glad to take her, really," said Louise enthusiastically.

Never one to give up without a fight, I pressed on. "Mom, you know as well as I do that Bitsey will probably do something awful and embarrass us." Little did I know that this was exactly what was going to happen.

"Ernie," said Mom sternly, "you heard my terms . . . take her or stay here."

Well, within minutes Louise and I, changed into our new swimsuits, were heading toward the beach with the colossal pain of all time happily following along behind us.

"Claudie wanted to go swimming with us, Ernie," whined the bathing beauty.

Trying very hard to be patient, I told her, "Now Bitsey, Mom explained to you that no animals are allowed on the beach. Besides, I don't think Claude wants to leave the cottage. He's probably very happy to stay . . . "

Louise interrupted my monologue by nudging me on the back and saying in a very low voice, "Looooook over there!"

By this time we had reached the beach. Louise was looking in the direction of the lifeguard's station. There stood the most beautiful boy that I had ever laid eyes on, probably the most beautiful boy in the whole U.S. of A., if not the entire world!

"Geez, Louise," I gasped.

"I think I'm going to faint," whispered Louise in a low voice.

"Boy, isn't he cute, though," I responded, "and look at those muscles. I'm going right out into the lake and drown so HE can rescue me."

We both giggled at the thought of this and almost fell into each other, since we both had our eyes glued to Mr. Beautiful.

"Wow," said Louise, "this vacation is going to be even better than I thought it would be."

"Oh, wow, you know it," I said.

"Let's put our towels here on the sand and go for a swim," I suggested.

"Okay," agreed Louise as we placed them side by side close enough so that we could watch Mr. Beautiful.

"Is Mr. Beautiful looking over here?" I asked Louise since I was afraid to look.

"No," she sighed, as she pretended to be looking for something just beyond the lifeguard's station. Louise is never obvious in these matters.

"Bitsey swimming," hollered the twerp.

"What do you think his name is?" I ignored the dauntless swimmer.

"Well, I guess we'll just have to find out, won't we?" smiled Louise. Then with a dramatic gesture, she placed her hand over her heart and quietly crooned, "In think I'm in *love* with Mr. Beautiful." That set us off into gales of laughter.

"Bitsey swimming," came the well-known insistent voice.

"Yes," I agreed. "Bitsey swim here. Louise and I are going out a little farther where it's deeper."

Looking at Louise, I added, "Maybe we'll have a cramp and Mr. Beautiful will have to come to our rescue." This set us off

41

into another laughing fit so that we had to hold on to each other as we walked into the water.

"Doesn't the water feel good?" asked Louise.

"Sure does," I agreed.

We were just lazily swimming around, sneaking glances at the lifeguard, getting really relaxed, so I was rudely jolted by the sound of a piercing scream from Bitsey. I turned in the direction of where we had left her and there she was standing right at the edge of the water. She was hopping up and down and screaming at the top, and I do mean the very top, of her lungs. Needless to say, I wasn't the only one to hear the little siren, for as I hurried through the water towards her, so did everyone else on the beach. By the time Louise and I reached her, she had gathered a very large crowd. The lifeguard, *our* lifeguard, was holding her and he managed to turn her loud shrieks into low murmurs.

"What's the matter?" he asked her.

"A stark . . . a stark was after me!" she said, in a quavering voice.

Mr. Beautiful looked puzzled. "A stark?"

"I think she means a "shark," " called a lady from the crowd.

"Oh . . . a shark," he repeated with a grin. Some of the people in the crowd began to snicker.

"That's what I said," said Bitsey.

"No, there aren't any sharks in Kickapoo Lake."

"There are too! I saw him! He tried to get me!"

"Show me where you saw the shark," humored the lifeguard.

"Right there," said Bitsey, pointing to the water. He walked over with her and she let out another shriek.

42

"There it is!"

A tiny little minnow swam between the feet of the lifeguard, so tiny that it wouldn't even be used for fishbait. He laughed—along with the rest of the crowd—then tried to explain what a minnow was to the scaredy-cat. I looked at Louise and she was laughing too.

"Oh, how embarrassing," I thought to myself. But another thought came into the back of my mind . . . about Mr. Beautiful. Now he was certain to notice me. After all, he had just rescued my little sister. If only I could think of some way, some humorous witty remark, perhaps, to carry off the whole embarrassing incident as a joke. But what happened next obliterated all such thoughts. I found that I really didn't know the meaning of the word, embarrassment—but I was soon to learn, with Bitsey as my teacher.

The crowd was beginning to disperse when the little shark-girl brought new meaning to "embarrassment."

"Can I have a minner, Mr. Bootiful?"

The lifeguard looked at her again in a puzzled way.

"Oh, no . . . not that . . . please not that," I groaned to myself as my face began to feel exceptionally warm.

"Come on, Louise, let's go," I begged. But it was too late.

"What did you call me?" asked the object of our affections.

"Mr. Bootiful," answered blab-all with a look of complete innocence.

"My name is Nick," he said with a smile. "Who ever told you to call me Mr. Beautiful?"

I would have gladly drowned at that moment without any regrets whatsoever. In fact, that's just where I wanted to be

. . . at the bottom, the very bottom of the lake, for I knew what was coming.

"Ernie said your name was Mr. Bootiful," answered the little twerp as she pointed directly to me.

By then my face must have been the shade of a fire engine. I slowly slid backwards into the water. My last wish before I was completely submerged was for a hungry "stark" to come along and make a hearty meal of Ernestine Cecelia Tubb.

CHAPTER FIVE

There was, of course, no "stark" that appeared to put me out of my misery—no such luck for poor old Ernie. I stayed submerged as long as I dared, and came up some distance from "Embarrassment Point." Louise and Bitsey were waiting for me and somehow we made it back to the cottage. I must have been in a daze because all I can remember is saying over and over again to Louise that I could never go swimming again while Mr. Beaut . . . Nick was on lifeguard duty. Louise kept reassuring me that although it was an awful experience, she was sure that everyone would forget all about it very soon. At least John Murphy hadn't been there to witness my humiliation. I was grateful about that. If he had been, he would never let anyone, especially me, forget about it. But, you say, naturally Bitsey apologized for what she did. Hah! Are you kidding? All she did was to babble on about wanting to get Claudie a pet stark so he wouldn't be so lonely back at the cottage without her.

In hopes of getting a little sympathy, some understanding, *and* being released from having to drag Bitsey everywhere I went, I told Mom and Dad the whole story when we got back.

That was a mistake. Mom did seem to understand, but Dad acted like he thought it was the funniest story he had every heard! Can you imagine . . . thinking the disgrace of his older daughter by his younger daughter *funny*. He had to sit down, he was laughing so hard. He just kept saying between gasps, "Oh, Ernie . . . oh, Ernie."

Well, the remainder of our first day at Kickapoo Lake was uneventful, at least in comparison . . . but that night . . . well that was something else! If I had to give a title to our first night in the cottage, it would be "That Great Wide-Awake Nightmare."

We were all (especially me) exhausted by our long, tiring day, so we decided to go to bed early that night to be fresh for tomorrow's adventures.

"Ernie, Louise," called Mom, "you two will sleep on the hide-a-bed and Bitsey on the sofa."

"Bitsey wanna sleep in the hide-and-seek bed!" demanded the great game player. I could just imagine the whole night of her hide-and-seek games. Nobody, but noboby else in the whole wide world plays hide-and-seek the way she does.

"Good grief, Bitsey . . . it's called a hide-a-bed . . . hide-a-bed . . . hide-a-bed," I kept repeating until Mom shot me another one of her looks.

"No, honey," explained Mom, "it's not a hide-and-seek bed. I said hide-a-bed. It's called that because the bed folds away so no one can see it during the day. Now, go brush your teeth and stop worrying about where everyone's sleeping."

Bitsey whined all the way to the bathroom, "Ernie gets to sleep on the hide-and-seek bed, but not Bitsey . . . poor Bitsey

. . . Mommie loves Ernie more than Bitsey . . . poor Bitsey . . . Mommie loves Ernie more than Bitsey. Poooor Bitsey."

Doesn't that just make you sick! If there's one thing I simply cannot stand it's someone who feels sorry for herself with no reason.

Dad was pulling out our sleeping place, saying, "You girls must be about the first ever to use this bed. It's so new that it doesn't want to unfold."

He was really struggling to get the bed (later to be known simply as the "death trap") open.

"We can help," offered Louise as she grabbed hold of the bed and began pulling. It was all that the three of us could do to pull it out so that it finally stayed flat. It didn't seem to want to stretch out.

"I guess the springs haven't been stretched enough," explained Dad, as it clicked in place at last. Little did we know that we had just assembled the first sleeping catapult in history!

"Claudie sleep with Bitsey," insisted sleeping beauty as she waddled from the bathroom to her bed. She was dragging Claude who looked resigned to being cuddled and half-smothered through the night . . . at least until the princess went to sleep.

"Which side do you want?" I asked Louise.

"Doesn't make any difference to me."

"Well, tonight, how about if I sleep on this side." I chose the side farthest away from you-know-who.

"Fine," answered Louise, and she slid under the covers on her side.

"Goodnight, girls," said Mom as she finished tucking in Bitsey and her reluctant sleeping companion, and headed in to her and Dad's bedroom.

"Goodnight," we all chorused.

"Don't let the bedbugs bite," came Dad's corny phrase.

Bedbugs . . . hah! I didn't know then that if there were any bedbugs they would be far too busy hanging onto the mattress for sheer survival to worry about dinner.

"Claudie can't go to sleep . . . nobody said goodnight to Claudie," complained a voice in the dark.

"Goodnight, Claudie," was heard from various parts of the cottage.

Peace and quiet settled down and I was just drifting off to sleep when a loud voice nearby called, "Claudie's thirsty."

"Well then, Claudie can just get up and get himself a drink of water from his bowl," called Dad.

"Claudie's too scared."

"Oh, sure," I whispered to Louise. "I just bet that it's *Claudie* who's scared."

"Honey," called Mom, "Claude is not afraid of the dark and if he's thirsty, he'll get himself a drink."

"Well," I continued to whisper to Louise, "It looks like old *Claude* will have to go to sleep thirsty."

Now that shows how the events of the day had unsettled me and affected my thinking. How could I have forgotten that Bitsey always gets her own way!

"Waaaaah!" cried Bitsey, "Claudie's thirsty. Poooor Claudie!"

"Ernie," Mom's voice sounded frazzled, and no wonder, "would you *please* supervise Claude *and* Bitsey in getting their go-to-bed drinks?"

"I should have known! Slave Ernie at your Service!" I said loud enough for Bitsey to hear, but not so loud that Mom could hear. I got the caravan together and herded them to the kitchen where I flicked on the light.

"Here, your highness . . . do you suppose that *now* you and your *scaredy cat* can manage to get a drink by yourselves?"

There came a warning "Ernie" from my parent's room, so I must have been talking louder than I realized. It was hard to believe that after they knew what I had been through that day, they would expect me to shoulder further abuse. Little did I know then, that it was just beginning.

"Claudie say 'sank you,'" tweeted the birdbrain as she bounced back to bed leaving me standing barefoot in the kitchen. I turned off the light and plodded back to bed.

"Did you ever?" I whispered.

"Oh, she's so funny . . . so cute with her Claudie," giggled Louise.

"Hm," I thought, "she might not think 'funny' or 'cute' if she had to get out of bed."

"You know what I wonder?" whispered Louise.

"No, what?"

"I wonder what Mr. Beautiful is doing right now."

"Good grief, Louise, how could you remind me of him when I'm trying to get to sleep? I'll probably have nightmares about him laughing at me."

"Oh, by tomorrow he won't even remember anything about it."

"Well, if he doesn't, I'm sure the bigmouth Bitsey will remind him! Maybe I'll just not go swimming again."

49

"Oh, Ernie, things will look better in the morning." comforted Louise.

Well, I doubted that, but I was tired so I simply told Louise goodnight and rolled over in my second attempt to get some sleep.

I was lying there thinking about how awful our first day had been and hoping that it wasn't a preview of the whole week, when I heard a very low squeaking sound. I couldn't place it at first and then when I heard it again I knew what it was— the sound a shoe makes on bare wood.

I was about to turn blue from holding my breath when I heard it for the third time. I exhaled as quietly as I could and nudged Louise.

She had already dozed off because she started and said in a normal voice, "What's the matter?"

"Shhhh!" I cautioned in a whisper. "There's someone or something in this room. I keep hearing a squeaking sound— listen."

We lay there listening and the squeak came again.

"Did you hear that?"

"Yes," answered Louise in a shaky voice. "What do you think it is?"

"I don't know. Do you think . . ." I began, but stopped immediately when the squeak sounded again . . . much louder than before. Louise grabbed my hand. Just as she did we heard another squeak, accompanied by a loud groan . . . and the bed moved.

"There's something under our bed!" cried Louise, too scared now to whisper.

We were both on the verge of complete hysteria when we heard a loud SNAP followed by various squeaking and groaning sounds. As Louise and I let out a mixture of screams and gasps, the bed lurched violently and folded up!

We weren't the only ones who were scared, because Bitsey let out a piercing scream that must have been heard back in Pleasant Valley.

I could hear Mom and Dad rushing in, hollering, "Bitsey, Ernie, Louise . . . what's the matter?"

When they turned the lights on, they found Bitsey standing in the middle of her bed with her eyes tightly closed and her mouth open so wide that it could have passed for Mammoth Cave. She held Claude in such a tight clutch that he looked like he was being strangled. Mom and Dad ran to her and tried to calm her down—or at least shut her up. It was only then they looked for Louise and me. I should say what was left of Louise and me. Louise was on the floor, half under the collapsed bed, having been thrown clear in its flight. But, you might wonder, where was Ernie? Had she also been thrown clear? No, she had not! Was she on top of the "death trap"? No, she was not there either! Oh, no, not poor old Ernie. Well, you may keep wondering, where else could she be? If you haven't already guessed, let me tell you. Poor old Ernie was caught *inside*—you heard me—*inside* the collapsed bed. I must have looked like a hot dog in a bun.

The only part of me that was visible was a little section of my forehead and one of my eyes. I lay there thinking what a fitting ending to such a perfect day, when Dad saw my eye and bounded over to pry me loose. It seemed that there was a snap on the back of the bed, that we had neglected to catch after pulling it out and that's what caused it to whip shut taking me with it. It was a real giant trap-in-the-box.

"Ernie, Ernie, are you alright?" asked my worried Dad.

"I think so," I said slowly, examining my arms and legs. "Oh, but my head hurts."

"Where, honey?" asked Mom, who had rushed over to the scene of the accident with Bitsey still in her arms.

"Here," I said, pointing to my eye.

"Oh, yes, it's starting to swell. Pete, quick get some ice."

Dad hurried to the refrigerator and quickly brought back some ice wrapped in a paper towel.

"Ouch," I groaned as he placed it on my head above my eye.

"It doesn't look too bad," he said, "but I imagine you'll have a shiner by morning."

"Oh, no," I groaned again. The thought of a black eye hurt worse than the pain in my head.

And then, to top everything off, Bitsey began to whine, "Ernie's playing in the hide-and-seek bed. Bad Ernie, won't let Bitsey and Claudie play. Bad old Ernie. Bad old Ernie."

CHAPTER SIX

Once the "death-trap" was put back together again, this time with the catch *securely* fastened, all of the sleepy inhabitants of the little cottage on Waterfront Drive settled down once again. This time I managed to get a night's rest without any interruptions. When I woke up the next morning, I felt pretty good, considering what I had been through the night before. The only reminder of the unfortunate accident was a slight headache over one eye, I *thought* that was the only reminder—until I saw a sight in the bathroom mirror that I really wasn't prepared to see.

"Oh, no," I wailed. "Oh, how awful!"

Louise rushed in to see what was the matter.

"Oh, gosh, Ernie . . ." as she stared at me, "you have got one *super* black eye!"

Now that's just what I needed—a comforting remark from my best friend. Sometimes Louise is just too painfully honest.

"Geez, Louise, there's nothing *super* about it. Just look at it. I hate it. It is a big, ugly, black mess!"

Mom stuck her head in to see what all of the groaning and

moaning was about.

"Oh, honey, that's too bad. Does it hurt?"

"Only when I look at it—but I do have a headache." I thought I might as well get as much sympathy as I could.

"Oh, Ernie," said Dad, as he joined the little group of sightseers crowding into the tiny bathroom, "it will soon fade. Don't fuss so much about it." So much for the sympathy.

I was beginning to feel like the star attraction at a side show and thought maybe I should begin selling admission tickets.

"How *soon* is soon?" I asked, pinning Dad down to a definite answer.

"Oh . . . I'd guess that it will probably be all gone at least by the time we get back home."

"BY THE TIME WE GET BACK HOME!!!" I exploded. "That's almost a whole week . . . that's the rest of our time here. You mean that I have to go around looking like one-half of a raccoon all that time!" I was just about upset enough to cry.

"Well . . . you *could* put a paper bag over your head," suggested Dad, with a grin.

I *was* upset enough to cry and must have looked it.

"Now, Pete," warned Mom, "this is no time for jokes."

"Oh, Ernie, I'm sorry," apologized Dad, "but you're stuck with it so you might as well make the best of it and laugh at it."

With that, the black-eye-viewers group broke up and left the side-show stage for the living room. I thought to myself, "That's fine for him to say. He doesn't have to face everyone looking like some kind of freak." I must admit that the main "everyone" to enter my mind was Mr. Beaut . . . Nick.

"Ernie," started Bitsey. Then she stopped and looked at me

54

with her forehead wrinkled in thought.

"Ernie," she began again, now all smiles. "You know something, Ernie?"

Usually her "you know something" questions annoy me so much that I don't even bother to answer her, but this morning I was too discouraged to care.

"Alright, what?"

"You've got two different colored eyes . . . just like Claudie."

"No, Bitsey," I patiently explained. "Claudie has one green eye and one blue eye. I hurt my eye last night, and now it's turned black."

"No, it's not turned back, it's right there. I can see it. But it's a funny color. Claudie's eyes are prettier."

"Turned black . . . BLACK, not *back*!"

"Ernie should be more careful not to turn back her eye," she said, with a knowing nod in my direction.

"Just give up," I told myself. "Don't waste your breath."

Considering everything that happened to me on our first day at Kickapoo Lake, I was beginning to dread the rest of our vacation. Surprisingly enough, though, Ernestine Cecelia Tubb's luck seemed to change from bad to good and no more disasters happened for the next few days. Nick seemed to have forgotten about the "Mr. Beautiful" episode and was very friendly to Louise and me, my eye had turned from black to a greenish-purple, Louise and I were both getting great tans, I was really relaxing and enjoying myself. In fact, the "uneventfulness" of those days made me think that the worst was over . . . I should have known better!

Our first (and last) Friday arrived, and with it many more

people coming for the weekend. The beach was much more crowded now and I was thankful that Bitsey had done her "stark" routine when she did and not today. Louise and I had found a place on the beach and were sunning ourselves and listening to her transister radio when I heard the barking of a dog off in the distance.

"Just listen to that, Louise. Someone brought a dog on the beach. These weekenders . . . they don't know the rules." By now Louise and I felt like old-timers and were really put out by having to share *our* beach with all of the newcomers. It was such a nuisance—after all, they were nothing but tourists.

"I guess we're going to have to watch where we step from now on," laughed Louise.

I turned over on my back, chuckling at Louise's clever remark. We both lay there without talking, just listening to the music. I remember I was thinking how restful it all was . . . even with the tourists . . . when it happened!

"Arf, arf . . . Hi, Ernie . . . arf, arf."

I lay there very still, wondering how I could be so wide awake and still be having a bad dream. "Don't move a muscle," I told myself, "and the dream will go away."

"ARF, ARF . . . Pant, pant . . . HI, ERNIE," the dream hadn't gone away, It just became closer and louder.

Without opening an eye, I said resignedly, "Hello, Chester."

"Gosh, Ernie . . . pant, pant . . . how'd you know it was me . . . bow, wow."

"Because, Chester," I said, through closed eyes and clenched teeth, "it was only a matter of time for the cow who turned into a chicken to become a dog."

"Gee, you sure are smart, Ernie," commented the great imitator. Then he let out a growl so fierce that I almost jumped off my towel.

"For heaven's sake, Chester, quiet down."

"Yes, down boy," giggled Louise, who had been listening in silent awe until now.

"Oh, Louise," I moaned, "that's awful." Then I turned back to the object of our attention. "Chester, what on earth are *you* doing *here*?"

"Bow wow, we came with the Murphys and are staying with them at their cottage on Waterfront Drive." Then he got down on all fours and began digging a hole in the sand, dog fashion.

"Oh, no ... " I groaned. "Louise, did you hear that?"

"Yes," Louise groaned back. "Chester, did John come with his parents?"

"Yes, arf, arf," he answered as he pretended to drop a bone in the hole and furiously covered it up.

"Wouldn't you know it," I said, looking at Louise. "Just when things were improving. I'd forgotten that the Murphys had a cottage here ... *and* on Waterfront Drive ... of all places."

"Maybe we can avoid him," suggested Louise.

"There's as much chance of that as there is that Chester will make sense one of these days," I said. "In all my twelve years I have yet to be able to avoid that colossal drip."

I should say right here and now that John Murphy, variously know as the Murphy-the-Mouth, Megaphone-Mouth Murphy, or just plain dope, as the occasion demanded, does nothing but pester and tease me in and out of school every chance he gets. He just never lets up. It got really bad last year with my parents' switching jobs. There was just no end to his stupid comments then.

"Bow wow . . . Albert came too," said our canine informer.

"Albert will never come to," I informed our canine.

Louise gave me a knowing look. "Oh, isn't that great. Just what John needs . . . one of his dim-witted cronies to show off in front of."

"Bow wow . . . your eye looks funny, Ernie. What happened to it?"

"Oh, it's just some new eye make-up I'm trying, Chester," I said sweetly.

"Sure makes your eye a pretty green, arf, arf. You oughta put it on your other eye, too, arf, arf, arf," said the dog as he went trotting on all fours.

"Honestly . . . he will believe anything," I said to Louise.

"Ernie, tell me," said Louise, "why does Chester pretend to be different animals?"

"I don't know, Louise. I doubt that even Chester knows. Why not ask him? Chester . . ." I hollered, but it was too late. Fido was already sniffing around the lifeguard's post!

I looked around cautiously, half expecting to see John Murphy looking back at me with that disgusting smirk on his face.

"Louise, do you think he's here on the beach already?"

She looked around. "I don't see him, but let's not take any chances. Why don't we take out the rowboat?"

"That's a great idea," I agreed."If old bigmouth and his sidekick aren't here already, they probably will be any minute."

We quickly gathered up our things and hurried off towards

the cottage, keeping a wary eye out for you-know-who.

"Hi, girls," called Mom as we walked by the cottage. "Leaving the beach so soon?"

"We're going to go out in the rowboat," I yelled.

"Well, be careful," she warned.

Her remark was followed by scurrying noises accompanied by screams of "Me, too, me too. I wanna go robie . . . I wanna go robie."

I knew it. We should have never told Mom what we were going to do, because you can just guess what she said next, can't you?

"Ernie, please take . . ."

"Bitsey with you," I finished for her. I figured there was no use in arguing any more, so I simply said, "Okay."

This must have caught Mom off guard because she came back with, "Now Ernie, I'm sure she'll be good and she's been here all morning with . . ." she stopped in mid-sentence. "Honey, did you say okay?"

"That's right."

While Mom was still staring, Bitsey slammed open the screen door and made a mad dash for the boat. As the Olympic runner streaked past us, I caught a glimpse of a terrified-looking Claude clutched under one arm.

"Be sure Bitsey puts on her lifejacket . . . and thanks Ernie," Mom smiled.

Bitsey was already sitting on her majesty's throne at the front of the boat when we got there. She was struggling with her lifejacket with one hand while keeping a tight grip on Claude with the other.

"Here, sweetie," said Louise, "let me help you with that lifejacket."

"Sank you, Wheez," returned the gracious queen. "Claudie needs a lifejacket too."

"Oh, brother," I thought, I could just picture our long-suffering Claude in a lifejacket.

"Claude really doesn't need a lifejacket of his own, Bitsey. That's because he has you to look after him." Louise is so patient with her.

This did seem to please the little princess and no more was said about Claude's life being in peril.

"Don't step on the bailing can," I warned Louise.

She was so busy with Bitsey that she almost crunched our survival kit. You see, the rowboat came with the cottage, but let me tell you, it was no big deal. It looked to be about fifty years old and had been painted and repainted many times. We knew this because the paint had chipped and peeled so much that it now was all the colors of a rainbow. As you have probably already guessed from our survival kit, The Queen Elizabeth, as it was called, also leaked . . . just a little. Yes, that's right. The person not rowing had to take the can and bail out the water every so often. No matter what, it was a whale of a lot better than running afoul of the Mighty-Mouth who was no doubt on the beach this very minute looking for yours truly.

Rover wouldn't have lost any time barking our presence.

"Giddy-up!" shrieked the Queen of the Nile.

"Good grief, Bitsey, giddy-up is for riding on horses, not boats." I might just as well have been talking to one of the oars.

"Giddy-up, giddy-up," she repeated, as Claude gave me a backward glance that spelled pure disgust . . . mixed with a bit of terror.

In between "giddy-ups" I managed to hear Louise say, "I'll push off, Ernie, if you want to begin rowing."

"Okay," I hollered back as I fitted the oars into the oarlocks. Unfortunately, the oarlocks were as worn as the rest of the boats and it was a real job to keep the oars from continuously slipping out.

"We're off!" shouted Louise, as she pushed off and jumped in. We were off, alright . . . off into an adventure that I would not soon, it ever, be able to forget.

CHAPTER SEVEN

As the boat heaved away from the dock, thanks to Louise's great push, our river queen slowed down her giddy-up song so that now it more resembled a giddy-up hiccough.

"Isn't this peaceful?" Louise asked, as we glided (more or less) along the lake. "The lap of the waves against the boat, the sparkle of the sun on the water. Gee, I wish we could stay here forever."

"Giddy-up."

"It is nice," I agreed, ignoring the hiccough. "But do you know what would make it perfect . . . absolutely perfect?"

"Of course," laughed Louise, "Nick . . . Nick ought to be here with us."

"Right again," I told her. "If only Nick were here."

"Giddy-up."

"Well, maybe not perfect, but close," I said, glaring at our little directional signal.

"Don't forget to bail, we don't want to capsize," I reminded Louise.

"You're doing a lot better rowing than our first time out,"

complimented Louise.

"Giddy-up."

"I sure hope so," I laughed, "remember how we kept going around in circles? At least we now go in zig-zag fashion."

"Bitsey wanno go ziggy-zat . . . ziggy-zat," commanded mixed-up mouth, bouncing up and down on her throne causing a look of terrible seasickness to appear on Claude's face, and the boat to veer from side to side. It's hard to describe my exact emotions about the possibility of having a seasick cat in a boat with us . . . let me just say I felt a bit queasy myself over that prospect.

I had to yell at her. "Bitsey, stop that bouncing. It's hard enough to keep this boat going in one direction without you messing it up. And besides, you're making Claude sick."

Bitsey settled down a bit, but couldn't restrain a little bounce every now and then. Claude gradually looked somewhat less green and that made me feel better.

"Oh, look," called Louise, "we're getting near the spot where all the lilypads are," and she pointed on ahead. "Let's go over there."

"That's a good idea," I said, heading in that direction as best I could.

We must have been quite a sight as we made our way in a slowly-weaving zig-zag pattern across the lake. Bounce, row, row, bail . . . bounce, row, row, bail . . . interrupted by cries of "Giddy-up." I was just hoping if anyone *was* watching, it was not Murphy.

As we neared the backwater area that was filled with lily-pads, the queen of the lake became terribly excited.

"Claudie wants a litty," she squealed.

"Oh, yeah . . . I'm sure *Claudie* wants a lily," I shot back. "And it's LILY . . . LILY."

"That right, Claudie wants a litty, and Claudie wants it NOW!" came her strident demand.

Louise, the peacemaker, broke in, saying, "Bitsey, why don't we wait until we get in a ways. That's where the big lilies are."

"Okay, if you say so, Wheez." Bitsey was very cooperative for once. "As long as it's alright with Claudie."

"Boy," I thought to myself, "Louise sure has a way with the little dingbat. She never does what I ask her to do."

As I rowed us farther into the backwater area, the lilypads became thicker and the water more shallow.

"Claudie wants THAT litty," shouted you-know-who as she pointed to a large lily still some distance away.

"Well, then," I replied as I struggled with the oars, which seemed to be getting heavier, "*Claudie* can just swim over there and get THAT litty . . . I mean, lily."

"You told me that Claudie can't swim. You said no cats can swim. You want Claudie to be drowned," whined the little twerp.

"Oh, good heavens . . ." I began.

Loiuse interrupted, "Now, now, I think we can get it." Then the great humanitarian went on, "Give me one of those oars, Ernie. I think we could make headway better by poling and pushing our way now that the water's getting so shallow."

"Sounds good to me," I responded, glad to be getting rid of one of the oars. I was getting plenty tired from all that rowing.

Louise and I stood in the boat, each of us carefully pushing an oar into the soft lake bottom to move us along. We made our way ever so slowly over to where the big litty grew ... *Claudie's* lily. We were almost there, when we heard a loud scraping noise and at the same time we were badly jolted to a halt.

"What was that?" I asked.

"Maybe it's a stark," a big-eyed Bitsey spoke in hushed tones. "Oh, please Ernie, Wheez ... don't let the stark get poor Claudie."

"It can't be a SHARK, Bitsey," I said, repeating, SHARK, even though I knew it would do no good.

"It must be an old stump of a dead tree," guessed Louise. "We passed several others that were sticking out of the water on our way over here."

"Well, whatever it is, I think we're stuck on it."

"Claudie want his litty," demanded the little creep, not caring that we were marooned in the middle of nowhere ... or maybe she is just too much of a dingbat to realize what was going on.

Well, I could see that it was time for Ernestine Cecelia Tubb to take control. If I do say so myself, I really am at my best in an emergency situation ... cool, calm, and fully in charge of my thoughts and emotions.

"Louise," I ordered, "you go to the front of the boat and I'll work from the rear. Bitsey ... not one word out of you while Louise and I attempt to deliver us from this nightmare."

Bitsey turned her head to listen for further instructions. It was easy to see that she was terribly impressed with my "take charge" manner. I kind of impressed myself too with being so well-organized. Claude's eyes glinted at me, his tail switched, and he let out one low hiss. Maybe for him, that's being impressed. Who knows?

"Alright, Louise," continued the command general, "when I count to three we will both push on our oars at the same time."

"Gotcha," agreed my second-in-command.

"One . . . two . . ."

"Giddy-up," whispered Bitsey.

"Three!"

I felt the sensation of movement, but it wasn't the boat moving. It didn't budge an inch, but my oar sunk down into the lake bottom at least one foot.

"Claudie wants his litty," cried her highness.

I decided to ignore her insubordination to my "be quiet" orders and said, "Louise, let's try again . . . but this time, give it everything you've got!"

"I'll do my best," said Louise, bracing her foot against the middle seat.

"Ready now, here we go," I ordered. "ONE . . ."

"Giddy-up."

"TWO . . ."

"GIDDY-UP."

"Hiss."

"THREE!"

Now, you're simply not going to believe what happened on the count of three. I mean, so many things happened all at the same time, that even I, Ernestine Cecelia Tubb, have a hard time believing it . . . and I was there . . . oh, was I *ever there!* As Louise and I expended all of our combined strength in a mighty push, we caused the boat to lurch forward in freedom. This, in turn, created a chain of events that I'm sure could go down in the *Guinness Book of Records.*

First, my oar sunk even deeper into the lake bottom and I was thrown completely off-balance.

Second, since I was thrown off-balance backwards, instead of forwards mind you, I clutched at the only thing left to hold onto . . . my oar.

Third, the boat moved swiftly out from under me, leaving me hanging on the oar like one of those toy monkeys on a stick.

Fourth, the jolt scared Bitsey who jumped up in the air waving her hands over her head, consequently relinquishing her hold on Claude.

Fifth, this resulted in Claude being catapulted from the boat in what was probably the first cat-swan-dive ever, and he landed right in the middle of the lilypads of Kickapoo lake.

Sixth, the result of the last two events caused complete hysteria in Bitsey. I mean, she really lost it!

"Claudie . . . Claudie!" she was screaming at the top of her lungs.

"I'll get him . . ." shouted Louise as the boat moved forward toward a panic-stricken Claude who was frantically treading water, and not liking it one bit. He must have surfaced under his large "litty" pad because it was draped over his head rather like a bonnet. It was quite a charming sight, really.

All of this was going on, mind you, while poor old Ernie was clinging desperately to the oar.

"Help!" I yelled, but no one heard me over Bitsey's screaming and Louise's shouting. I tried again as I slowly began to slide down the length of the wet, slippery oar into the water.

"Help!"

I could see Louise lift a dripping Claude from the water . . . lilypad and all . . . and place him in the lap of the screaming banshee. Taking advantage of this slight lull in the screaming/shouting hysteria, I called one more time, "Heeeeelp!" as I slid lower and lower into the water.

"Oh, no!" Louise cried, as she turned away from comforting the all-but-for-her-bereaved. "Hold, on, Ernie, hold on. I'll be right there!"

I could see that Louise was making a Herculean effort to reach me but by now my descent down the oar was complete, and I was standing waist deep in the water with both of my feet mired in the mucky bottom!

"Louise, Louise," I shouted, "get me out of here. Get me out of here, NOW!"

"Here," she called, "grab hold of my oar."

I did as she told me, but that was unfortunate. That was absolutely *not* the thing to do, as I discovered about a second too late. When I let go my hold on my "stable" oar for her "unstable" one, I not only became mired more deeply in the muck, I also lost my balance. This caused me to take a most ungraceful nose dive into the lilypads! By the time I had regained my balance and came up for air . . . screaming . . . the back of the boat was right next to me, and Louise was hanging over it reaching out her hands.

"Ernie," she shouted, as she grabbed hold of me. "Ernie, are you alright?"

"I gueth tho," I tried to answer, but discovered that it's rather difficult to speak clearly with a large lilypad in your mouth.

With Louise's help and great exertion on my part, I soon managed to crawl back into the boat. I collapsed on the bottom and just sprawled there, feeling like a mucky-footed half-drowned rat.

As I lay there thinking how good it was just to be alive, Bitsey showed her colossal nerve and lack of good sense by tugging on my sleeve and whining, "Ernie, Ernie, you brought up the wrong litty. Claudie wanted that bigger one over there! Wait till I tell Mommy that bad old Ernie wouldn't get Claudie the litty pad he wanted!"

CHAPTER EIGHT

"Who wants to try out the Water Whip with me?" asked Dad as we finished washing the lunch dishes.

There was an immediate chorus of yeses from Louise, Bitsey and me. Only Mom was silent, then she said, "Oh, Pete, do you think you really should?"

"Good heavens, why not? What could possibly happen to anyone on the Water Whip? It's not a dangerous ride."

Now right then, right then was the *exact moment* that Ernestine Cecelia Tubb should have stopped dead in her tracks to spend a considerable amount of time pondering that question. But no . . . good old Ernie, being the unsuspecting, good trouper she is, not wanting to spoil anyone's fun, let herself be swept along with the group in a thorough endorsement of the plan.

Looking back now, I see that I should have realized that cloud brimming over with imminent disaster was still hanging over my head. Yesterday's rowboat calamity should have given me irrefutable proof of that.

"Claudie wants to go down Walter's Dip, too."

"Oh, sure," I said, sarcastically, remembering his swandive into the lilypads. "Claude really liked his swim yesterday, didn't he?"

I couldn't believe what the little cat-lover did next. She actually stood there *thinking* about what I had said. Then she told a rather anxious-looking Claude, "you better stay here and I'll tell you all about it when I get back. Okay, Claudie? Okay, that's what we'll do." Claudie walked away, looking as relieved as a cat possibly can.

"Will wonders never cease!" I thought to myself, "The little birdbrain *can* think," but I knew better than to express my astonishment out loud.

I noticed Mom and Dad exchanging pleased looks over Bitsey's head.

Mom told Bitsey, "I'll stay here with Claude and keep him company."

"Oh, come on, Helen," coaxed Dad, "go with us."

"Not on your life . . . or *my* life as I think the case would be! I'm not so sure that Bitsey should go either."

"Waaaaaa," wailed the bawl-baby. "Waaaaaa." Boy, oh boy, what a waterworks. She sure can turn on the tears at a moment's notice.

"It'll be alright, honey," said Dad, trying to make himself heard over Bitsey's crying . . . and that wasn't easy. "I'll keep her with me all of the time."

"Well . . . I suppose she'll be alright," agreed Mom.

Would you believe that at the very instant Bitsey heard those words her wailing ceased immediately. A big smile lit up her face, and she hopped up and down, chanting, "Bitsey going

71

... Bitsey going!" Well ... that's our little "I-know-how-to-get-anything-I-want" girl.

"Now, please be careful," warned Mom.

"Oh, for goodness sakes, Helen. We will, we will," grumbled Dad as we started out of the cottage to walk the three blocks to the Water Whip. We already had our bathing suits on, so the eager band of prospective "water whippers" didn't have to waste any precious time changing.

As we came closer to the Water Whip, we could hear the shouts of laughter of the riders. Soon we could see the huge mountain with its maze of spillways filled with both kids and adults rushing down them.

We stood at the foot of the structure looking up for a minute.

"Oh, gosh," said Louise, "it sure looks a lot higher than it did from the car window, doesn't it?"

"Bitsey first ... Bitsey first!" shouted the daredevil.

"No, no," said Dad, "I'll take you one at a time to show you how to maneuver yourselves on the mats. Louise, you come with me first."

I figured the waterworks would be turned on again, but Bitsey didn't make a sound. She must have sensed that Dad meant business, so she didn't pull her crying act again.

"Thanks, Mr. Tubb," said Louise, "but I think I'd rather stay here with Bitsey and watch while you and Ernie come down. Besides I need some time to get my nerve up."

"Why sure," said Dad. "How about it, Ernie ... do you want to go first?"

"Are you sure you don't want to?" I asked Louise, hoping that her answer would be no.

"Really, Ernie. I just want to watch for a while. I'll ride down after you do."

"Okay," I answered quickly before she had a chance to change her mind and/or before Bitsey had a chance to begin her wailing routine. I guess I didn't have to worry about Bitsey, though, for she seemed absolutely enthralled with just watching the people streak down the various slides.

Dad paid for an hour's riding time for each of us. "I'll pay for more time if we decide to stay longer."

As we went through the gate, we each picked up a mat on which we were supposed to sit during the entire ride . . . all except Bitsey who would come down with Dad.

"Now then, Bitsey, you stay with Louise right here by the splash-down pool and watch for us." Bitsey nodded her head solemnly at Dad's instructions . . . so overwhelmed by the enormity of the giant waterway that her mouth stayed closed for once.

One after another of the riders was spilling into the pool as their ride down the mountain ended in loud splashes and high waves.

"Gosh, look at that," Louise's voice echoed her apprehension. "They sure do come down fast!"

"Oh, yes," beamed Dad. "It does look like fun, doesn't it? Come on, Ernie, let's show them how the Tubbs do it."

I could tell by Louise's comment and the growing fearful expression on Bitsey's face that they felt as I was beginning to feel . . . that maybe this wasn't such a hot idea after all. But Dad was already trudging up the path on his way into outer space, so, in response to his "Hurry up, Ernie," his obedient servant began her walk into danger.

Well, if I thought the mountain looked high from down below . . . let me tell you . . . it looked three times as high from the top.

"Just look at all those twists and turns. Boy, there's even a tunnel," Dad almost glowed in his enthusiasm.

"Yeah," was my somewhat less-than-enthusiastic response. Dad was so excited about the prospect of being whisked down the water slide that he didn't even notice. I don't mind telling you that this was one time that I wished Bitsey *had* put up a fight. I was beginning to think that she might not be so dumb after all. She was standing very still beside Louise down at the splash-down pool. The two of them looked like miniature munchkins . . . to give you some idea how high we were. I lifted my hand in a feeble wave, but they didn't seem to notice. We were probably hidden from view by a cloud layer!

"Well," I told myself, "Ernestine Cecelia Tubb, no matter what dangers lurk ahead, you must be brave. You must not disappoint your father. He's expecting you to go with him to 'show them how the Tubbs do it,' and that's just what you're going to do."

So Ernie the lionhearted, with a complete disregard for her personal safety, carefully listened to her father and followed his instructions.

"Now watch how the others do it, Ernie. See, first you place the mat down just where the water comes out of those holes. Then sit on it and push off. Now, isn't that simple? Won't that be fun?"

74

"It looks simple enough. It should be fun. But that's what I thought about the rowboat ride . . . before we started."

"Oh, now, Ernie," he giggled, "that was something that wouldn't happen again in a million years."

"It seems like I've been through a lot of million years in my lifetime," I mused to myself.

Dad noticed my hesitation and said, "Come on, honey, what are you waiting for? Don't worry, I'll be right behind you."

Well, let me tell you right now that no truer words were ever spoken! He certainly was *right* behind me. What was about to happen to Ernie-the-Brave would henceforth and forever be known as "her narrow escape from death by form of squashing!"

As I cautiously lowered myself to the mat as I had seen the others do, Dad gave me a little shove, calling, "See you at the bottom."

Well, if you think I had time to even take one breath, you're wrong, very wrong. I shot down that first dip like I had been fired from a cannon. As I hit the first turn, I heard Dad shout, "Here I come." At least I assume that the last word was come . . I really didn't hear it because my head was half under water. That's right! The "little shove" Dad gave me put me a bit off balance, and when I hit that first turn I hit it hard. I must have leaned the wrong way because the next thing I knew my feet were where my head should have been . . . I was racing down on my back.

"Whoops!" I yelled, as I was sped through two more turns, one right after the other. Somewhere during this "S" turn, I did a complete somersault, ending up once more, thank goodness, in my original sitting position.

"Wow, lucky," I sighed. It was just then that I spotted a mat disappearing around the next turn at breakneck speed. "Gosh," I thought, "somebody's lost his mat." Then looking down to check mine I saw it was gone, "Oh, no," I cried, then I found that losing the mat wasn't all that bad because I began to move at a much slower pace. The next turn went much smoother. I remember thinking that if I was insane enough to try going down the raging rapids again I would not use a mat. I was feeling a lot better about the whole ride until I heard someone shout, "Look out!"

The sight that I saw on turning my head stunned me . . . it would have stunned anyone. Dad was barreling down on me like an uncontrolled steam roller. I tried to make myself go faster by pushing with my hands, but it was no use. The distance between us was narrowing fast. I hurried around another turn but the steam roller was gathering speed.

"Go faster," Dad yelled.

"I'm trying," I shouted as I twisted around to see him, not noticing the tunnel straight ahead. As I hit the dip and turn I did another somersault, ending up on my stomach. There I was now sliding down backwards!

From my new vantage point, I could see Dad frantically attempting to slow himself down, with a noticeable lack of success. In fact, he was gaining on me at top speed. Just as I braced myself for the unavoidable collision, the floor went out from under me and Dad's mat skimmed over my head.

"Am I doomed to die in a watery grave?" I wondered. But no, just then my feet touched solid surface. Then I realized

I had hit the pool at the bottom of the Water Whip.

"Ernie, Ernie . . . speak to me." Dad was awfully upset. I coughed and gasped awhile, then told him I would probably live. I would live to watch others risk life and limb on the Water Whip, but I would never, ever again go down it myself.

It was then that I became aware of all the people standing there. All of the people who had seen "how the Tubbs do it." Then I heard a familiar voice.

"Ho, ho, ho, if isn't the world's greatest water acrobat!"

I didn't have to turn around to know who it was. It was the voice of Megaphone-Mouth Murphy. How he always manages to find me at my most embarrassing times, I'll never understand.

"Hey, Albert . . . look what we found . . . Dolly Dolphin doing her tricks again.

"Hey, Hey," came Albert's brilliant response.

The two of them shut up when Dad turned around and glared at them. I knew, though, that it was only temporary. John and Albert would start in again at the first opportunity . . . and everybody who knew John and who knew me back in Pleasant Valley would be given the full details of Ernie's daring descent down Water Whip Mountain! How could I ever go back home and face them! If only I could stay at the lake forever . . . but no, life couldn't be that kind to poor old Ernie.

CHAPTER NINE

Louise had to elbow John and Albert out of her way to reach my side as I struggled out of the pool. She looked at me in amazement.

"Ernie, why did you ever decide to come down backwards on your very first time? And without a mat too!"

I would have told her that it was not only my *very first* time, it was also my very last time, but I was too dazed and weak to say anything. Dad followed me out of the pool carrying both of our mats.

"You seem to have lost this, Ernie."

"Oh, Dad," I managed to say, "I was scared to death that you were going to crash into me."

"So was I, honey, but luckily we reached the pool just in time," he smiled and patted me on the shoulder.

"Yeah, just in time for a near-drowning," I said to myself.

Then he turned to Louise, "Louise, the Water Whip is a bit rougher that I expected it to be. I think we should go down together on your first ride."

"That's okay with me, Mr. Tubb," nodded Louise.

Dad then stooped down and put his arm around Bitsey, "I'm sorry, sweetheart, but your mother was right. This ride isn't for you. You'll just have to stay here and watch the rest of us."

Even though I was still in a numb condition from the near-catastrophe, I braced myself for the tantrum that was inevitable, but nothing happened—no tears, no screams, not even a trembling lip. Bitsey just stood very still, completely mesmerized by the sight of the riders. She must not have moved a muscle since the start of my death-defying plunge. I wondered if she was growing roots. Dad paused for a minute waiting for the expected outburst, then looking a little surprised himself that it hadn't come, went on, "Ernie, if you'll stay here with your little sister, I'll take Louise down the slide."

"Glad to, Dad," I said in hearty agreement. Another surprised look from Dad. He didn't know what was going on with his girls. I would have agreed to anything, though, to avoid having to go down that demon run again.

"Wish me luck," called Louise as she hurried up the path after Dad. She sent me a pleading look, but I couldn't see any way out for her.

"Yeah, good luck," I hollered, really meaning it. Under my breath I muttered, "And you're certainly going to need it."

They had no sooner left than I heard, "Hey, Tubby, how'd you get that big shiner?" Yes, Laurel and Hardy were back.

Albert, following John's lead, asked, "Yeah, where'd you get that big shiner—run into a door?"

"Gosh, Albert," I said sweetly, "How do you ever think of such *clever* and *original* things to say!" Of course, my witty sarcasm went right over the dumbbell's head. In fact, he actually looked pleased with himself. Right then and there I figured that he and Chester had to be related!

"How's come you're wearing a new swimsuit instead of the bea-u-ti-ful black balloon-britches you wore last year?" That's Megaphone-Mouth—he has the memory of an elephant—never forgets a thing.

"Yeah," added Albert, "where's your black swimsuit?"

I decided to ignore their comments, having learned long ago that the best reaction to Murphy is no reaction at all. That didn't stop him though, he went right on.

"What's wrong with Tubby the Tuna?" chided Big-Mouth, "gotta stay here and take care of the little minnow?"

I just kept quiet and focused my eyes on the top of the mountain. I could understand why Louise hadn't returned my wave, everybody looked the same from this distance, particularly with the sun in your eyes.

"Hey, Albert, I bet Shamu the Whale is *afraid* to go down the Water Whip using a mat."

"For you information," I blurted out, completely forgetting my "no reaction" strategy, "I have used a mat on the way down," not adding "for three feet."

"Did you use it sitting up or lying down?" asked Murphy with what seemed to be genuine interest.

"Both," I answered, "and I have found it to be a very borring activity!" I was awfully glad I was not Pinocchio at the moment for my nose would have surely grown six yards. Little did John know that those were only two of the positions I was twisted into on my one and only excursion into fear.

I returned to my policy of ignoring them.

"Hey, Murph, let's get going. We're wasting time."

"Yeah, Albert, this sure is a WASTE OF TIME! I'll race you to the top."

"Thank goodness," I breathed, as they ran up the path.

Just then I heard a loud, "Ya-hoo!" and turned to see Dad and Louise come splashing into the pool. I might add that they were both sitting up on the mat *and smiling!*

Dad beamed as if he had built the whole thing himself. "Ernie," he said, "next time I want you to go down with me so *you* can get the hang of it."

I recoiled in terror at the sound of his words . . . "next time"!

"Louise," asked Dad, "do you think you can go down alone now?"

"Oh, sure, Mr. Tubb. Thanks for showing me how. It sure is fun."

"You know," he went on, "I really think Bitsey might be able to ride down with me. Ernie," he continued, looking around the pool, "where *is* Bitsey?"

"She's right . . ." I broked off in mid-sentence. She wasn't right here. In fact, she was nowhere to be seen. I started to panic.

"Well, she *has* to be right around here somewhere."

Dad gave me a very serious and worried look. "Ernie, you mean that you didn't keep an eye on her. You mean you let her wander off all by herself . . . especially in a crowd like this?"

"But, Dad, Murphy and Albert were teasing me about . . ."

Dad cut me off, "That's hardly any excuse for losing your baby sister," he growled. "Alright, since you didn't look after

Bitsey as I asked you to do, the three of us must fan out quickly to do a fast search around the grounds. Now hurry!"

Dad went directly in the direction of the refreshment stands, Louise toward the bathhouse, and I, too embarrassed to look at either one of them, began hunting for her around the pool area.

"Bitsey," I called, even though there was so much screaming, yelling, and splashing going on that she could have never heard me. "BITSEY!" I began to picture my little sister floating face-down in the water and a chill ran up my spine.

"Gee, I haven't really been very nice to her," I thought. Right then and there, I resolved that *if* we found her alive, I would make it all up to her, I mean, if we found her *breathing*, I would never say another bad word to her . . . or even about her. I would be dear Bitsey's devoted older sister, granting her every wish, her every whim for the rest of my life.

"Oh, please let her be alright," I said out loud, as I circled the pool. I was relieved not to find her there, but I began to be overcome with an ever increasing sense of despair.

"Where would be the next most dangerous place she could go?" I puzzled. "Yes, the mountain." I took off running as fast as my weak knees would allow, keeping a sharp lookout for her.

"What's the big hurry, Tubby?"

"John, Albert, have you seen Bitsey?"

"Wouldn't you know it, Albert! She's gone and lost her little sister *again.*"

"What do you mean, *again*?" I asked defensively.

"It seems to me there was a certain train ride last Christmas when she outsmarted you and gave you the slip."

Albert laughed, "Well, Murph, who can blame her for wanting to get away from this overgrown black-eyed Susan?"

I figured it was no use to expect any help from that pair, and raced on. Albert's stupid laugh, and various comments such as "Minnow is missing," " Tubby the Tuna loses sister," and "Bitsey bit the dust," floated after me.

I had almost reached the top of the mountain when the music on the loudspeaker stopped abruptly, and a man's voice said, "There is a little, lost girl here. She won't tell us her name, Ouch, stop that biting. You may claim her at the ticket office. And please hurry. Ouch, I said to stop that!"

People all over the mountain were laughing. It could be no other than our Bitsey, our own little mad-dog biter. I broke into a run down the path to the ticket office. On my way, I passed the two comedians who joined me in my dash downhill, saying, "Wait for us, we don't want to miss the fun!" I ran faster, trying to outdistance them.

Louise and Dad had gotten there before I did, and a teary-eyed Bitsey was resting in Dad's arms.

"Oh, Bitsey . . ." I panted, "Bitsey, where did you go?" I was close to crying myself, it was such a relief to see that she was unharmed.

"Bitsey wanna help her friend down the slide," she sniffled.

"Which friend is that?" asked a very relieved father.

"I guess she means me," said a familiar voice. It was Nick! I hadn't even noticed he was there, I concentrating so hard on Bitsey.

"I was a little late meeting my cousin and his friend at the Water Whip and was just starting in that direction," Nick explained, "when I noticed this little girl all by herself. I mean, I didn't see you, sir, or her mother, or either of her two sisters."

I heard Louise giggle at his last comment.

Dream boy went on, "Well, she came right up to me and told me I had to take her down Walter's Dip."

"Knew my friend wouldn't let no starked get me," claimed in our little runaway.

"I didn't know what she meant by Walter's Dip, so I asked where her family was, and she pointed at the Water Whip . . . so I brought her over here."

"Well, Nick," responded Dad, "I don't know how we can ever thank you enough."

"Hi, Nick," chuckled Murphy, who had been standing behind me taking it all in. "See you're keeping your record for rescues, even if it was only a minnow, and on dry land at that."

"Oh, hi, John, sorry I was late getting away to meet you."

"Oh, no," I thought, "Nick and John are cousins!"

Louise and I looked at each other with worried expressions. I knew we were thinking the same thing. Please, please, don't let John find out about the Mr. Beautiful ordeal.

'Well, I'd better be getting back to the beach," said Nick, as he shook Dad's hand. "Sorry John, but I have to get right back."

"Say thank you, Bitsey," Dad prompted. Another cold chill ran up my spine. Somehow I knew what was coming.

"Sank you, Mr. Bootiful."

I could have died. I didn't dare look at Louise. I knew she was dying too.

"Mr. Beautiful," echoed the Mouth. "Mr. Beautiful!"

"Yes," laughed Nick as he looked at Louise and me. "I guess she heard *that* from some other people."

"Mr. Beautiful!" chorused the two dopes, laughing so hard they almost fell down. Too bad they didn't fall down and break their big dumb mouths!

CHAPTER TEN

'Well, I certainly didn't expect you back so soon," called Mom from the lounge chair where she was sunning herself. "Did you have fun on the Water Whip?"

"Oh, Helen, you wouldn't believe what happened!"

"What do you mean, Pete . . . 'what happened?'" Mom's look of surprise turned to concern.

"Well, for starters, Ernie and I almost had an accident as we were sliding down."

"Almost!" I repeated in disbelief. "Mom, I was half-killed! I nearly drowned! That thing is a cross between a Mixmaster and a hurricane!"

"And then," continued Dad, giving me a glare, "Ernie lost Bitsey."

"Bitsey . . . lost!" Mom stiffened up in her lounge chair. "Oh, honey, come here."

Bitsey rushed into Mom's arms and her lower lip began to quiver and a big tear slid down her cheek.

Mom looked over her head, "Oh, Ernie, how could you!"

Isn't that just the limit! No reaction when her older

daughter narrowly escapes death, but let Bitsey-baby go for a little walk and it's panic express. I wondered if there was a child-abuse agency nearby.

Just then I remembered my vow back at the Water Whip when I was hunting for Bitsey, how I was going to make up not being very nice to her by becoming a devoted older sister. I knew there would never be a better time to begin. Besides, if I waited too long, I was certain that she would pull one of her dumb stunts to embarrass me again and spoil all of my good intentions.

Mom was crooning to Bitsey, "Everything's alright, now that you're back again, Bitsey. Everything's alright."

"Yes . . ." I began in a nice older sister fashion, "we are glad to have our Bitsey back. You must never go away again, dear Bitsey. It scares us all too much." My, those words sounded strange coming from my mouth.

Mom and Dad eyed me, they shrugged as they looked at each other.

"You can look surprised," I thought, "Why not? You are witnessing a reformed Ernestine Cecelia Tubb in action."

"Bitsey," I went on, "Honey, how would you like to play a game with Louise and me?"

I was on the receiving end of surprised stares again . . . even Louise seemed taken back by my invitation.

Bitsey stared at me a second, then shouted, "Yes . . ." She lost no time wiggling off Mom's lap and rushing into the cottage, presumably to get her favorite game, "Uncle Waddle's Barnyard."

She was back before I could blink an eye.

87

"Here," she stuck her barnyard game under my nose. "Play . . . play! You promised, you promised you'd play!"

"In a minute, honey," I told her in a loving manner. "Louise and I have to change into our shorts first. Then we'll play Bitsey's nice game."

"Play *now!*" came her insistent demand.

"Bitsey," Mom was talking to her, but still staring at me as if she couldn't believe her ears. "Ernie and Louise will play *after* they go in and change."

Now it was my turn to be surprised. Mom was actually taking *my* side instead of hers. Louise and I changed quickly. She looked at me in a funny way, but didn't ask why this new Ernie. I could see that she was curious but all she said was, "Gee, I really like your new shorts."

"Do you, Louise? I think the white and lavender combination does set off my new tan, don't you?"

She nodded in agreement, then suggested, "Why don't we play the game out on the dock so we can work on our tans at the same time."

"Sure, that's a great idea," I said.

So the three of us set out to play an exciting game of Uncle Waddle's Barnyard on our dock. Bitsey skipped along, singing, "Gonna play Waddy Widdle's Yarn, Waddy Widdle's Yarn."

"Isn't that clever of her to make up a different name?" I laughed.

"Honey," Mom called, "Ernie, you didn't bump your head coming down the slide, did you?"

"No, no, Mom. I'm fine now, but thanks for asking," I

replied. "I'm just so glad that my darling sister's alright. That's what's important."

My parents, Louise, *and* Bitsey gazed at me as if they were not really seeing their Ernie.

I smiled inwardly, thinking, "Well, you aren't. You are seeing the new Ernestine Cecelia Tubb. The showing-love-for-her-little-sister Ernestine Cecelia Tubb. The lavishing-care-on-her-little-sister Ernestine Cecelia Tubb. The extremely devoted older sister Ernestine Cecelia Tubb." Although I didn't suspect it then, the soon to be very unhappy Ernestine Cecelia Tubb!

We sat down at the end of the dock and laid out the gameboard and playing pieces. As you can guess, the game was quite simple . . . designed for three- and four-year-olds. Each player had a metal animal marker to move around the board and there was a stack of cards in the center. The playing procedure was that the first player turned over a card, looked at the picture of the animal on it, and made the appropriate sound for the animal. Then, if the sound was right, the player advanced one space. The player who first reached the barn was the winner. I figured that Chester would win this game hands down!

"Bitsey go first!" insisted my sweet little sister.

"Oh, yes, Bitsey, Ernie wants you to go first," I smiled.

She turned over the top card. It was a picture of a cow. "Oink . . . oink," she grunted.

'Sorry, honey, that's wrong. Louise, you're next."

"Bitsey's not wrong!" she shouted angrily.

"Honey," I explained, still trying to keep a smile on my face, "cows go moo, moo, not oink, oink. Your card was a cow."

"No . . . oink, oink, OINK!" she had turned up the volume.

There I sat, arguing about whether a cow goes moo, moo, or oink, oink. I couldn't believe it.

"Alright," I gave in, giving Loiuse a look that was bordering on exasperation, but still forcing a smile. "You can move your marker one step on the path to the barn."

"Two steps . . . Bitsey gets to move it two steps!"

"Now, why is that, dear?" I asked, my smile slowly taking on a glazed feeling.

"Cause Bitsey said oink, oink. Two times, two steps!" Her face took on that I'm-about-to-scream-if-I-don't-get-my-own-way look.

"Honey, sweetheart," I murmured through gritted teeth, "if that's true, then it means that if you said oink twenty times, you would win the game in one move."

Right, you guessed it. I didn't count the oinks, but Bitsey let loose with a run of them. She ended by throwing her marker up in the air and yelling, "I WIN. I WIN!"

Need I say where the marker went? Of course not. A stunned Bitsey watched as the little marker slowly sank to the bottom of Kickapoo Lake.

"Piggy, piggy. I want my piggy," she cried. You see, of all the different animals on the markers, Bitsey loves the pig best. I guess maybe she thought that since her marker was a pig, she was supposed to say oink.

"Gosh," said Louise, "we'll never find it down there."

"I WANT MY PIGGY!"

"Ernie will try to find it for you," I told her in my most

understanding older sister voice.

We all looked over the edge of the dock. Now, while the lake is fairly clear it isn't transparent, and you can't see to the bottom.

"I see piggy, piggy," called little sister.

"Where, honey?" asked big sister, the smile painted on her face by this time.

"There!" was her detailed direction.

"Do you see it, Louise?"

"I can't even see the bottom."

"Neither can I."

"I SEE IT!" said Bitsey, getting louder. "And it's right there. Piggy!"

She pointed to a spot in the water. I leaned over farther to try to see the dumb pig, but the water simply wasn't clear enough. "There, there, there," screamed my darling little sister, as she stamped her foot at each "there."

I looked at Louise, who just shrugged.

"Sweetums, are you *sure* you see it?" asked the devoted older sister, feeling her smile slowly slipping away.

"I SEE IT ... AND I WANT IT ...*NOW*!"

I figured that a kind-hearted, considerate older sister would take one last look, so I leaned over as far as I could to peer into the water.

At that moment, Bitsey let out a blood-curdling scream, "A stark, a stark, there's a stark!!!

Needless to say, her unexpected scream so unnerved and startled a certain older sister that she fell head-over-heels off the edge of the dock into Kickapoo Lake. If you'll remember

the new white and lavender shorts the older sister was wearing, it will help you understand the older sister's reaction.
When this well-meaning older sister came up for air, she was
more then just a teensy bit upset.

"Bitsey," I shouted, rubbing water out of my eyes, "you little dingbat! You . . . you . . . you . . . pest! I tried, I really
tried. I went along with playing your dumb game. I went
along with your stupid cow going oink. I would have even
gone along with letting you win the idiotic game by cheating
with all those oinks. But this is too much! Never, I mean never,
has anyone had to put up with such an impossible little sister
as you!"

Do you know what the ungrateful little creep did next? Well,
I'll tell you if you're sitting down and holding on to the arms
of your chair. She looked up at my parents, who had come
rushing at the sound of her screams, and said, "Ernie lost my
piggy . . . Ernie let the stark get my piggy . . ." then proceeded to cry her big tears.

CHAPTER ELEVEN

"Look, what's going on over there?" asked Mom, pointing to a small group of people assembled down at the beach.

It was Sunday, and we were driving past the beach on our way back to the cottage after enjoying Mom's treat of brunch at the Lake View Restaurant.

"Oh, yes," said Dad, "they're setting up for the festival. I meant to tell you about that."

"What is it?" I asked.

"Each Sunday there's a festival with food and games for everyone on the beach. It's centered around a different theme each week."

"Gee, that sounds like fun," commented Louise.

"It does, doesn't it?" continued Dad. "One of the check-out girls down at Haines Grocery Store was telling me about it when I picked up the groceries yesterday. I think she said that there are prizes for the game winners."

"I want my prize," shouted Bitsey, who up until now had been sitting quietly, listening.

"What do you mean, honey?" Mom asked, turning around

in her seat probably with the hope that she might understand her better if she could see her.

"I won a game, I want my prize."

"Bitsey, you little . . ." I had to catch myself, then went on, "you haven't even been to the festival yet. You can't have won a game!"

She began to pout. "Yes I did! I won Waddy Widdle's Yarn game and I want my prize."

The mention of that game was enough to make me sick at my stomach as I remembered how much of an effort I had made to be nice to her . . . and no one, particularly Bitsey . . . had even thanked me.

Mom turned around and started talking to Dad. "Why don't you explain it to her, Pete?"

Dad just laughed and said, "Now Bitsey, you'll just have to wait until later for your prize."

"Does that mean we get to go?" I hurried to ask in order to sidetrack the game player.

"Why sure . . . I think we should. Probably everyone from around the beach will be there."

"Oh, no," I groaned. "That means that those two you-know-who's will be there."

Louise nodded and said, "Oh, dear, John and Albert."

"Oh, girls, there'll be so many people there, I bet you won't even see them."

Boy, when Mom is wrong, she is really wrong. She didn't know it, but old Big-mouth's built-in radar system for finding me . . . and always at the wrong time . . . was going to be working at full capacity today.

"What time does it begin, Pete?"

"Oh, let me see. The games begin around three o'clock and dinner's served at six. Oh, yes, there was some mention of entertainment after the meal."

"Well then," said Mom, "let's make a day of it and get there by three."

Louise and I spent the next couple of hours rowing around the lake and there were no unfortunate incidents this time, I might add. We were smart enough not to take her highness along and to avoid any navigation into the "litty" pad-filled backwater. By the time we returned to the cottage, Mom, Dad and Bitsey were ready to leave for the beach.

"Are you girls ready for a Jamaican Holiday?" enthused Dad.

"Bitsey's ready for makin' doll of hay," chirped the no-sense kid.

I just rolled my eyes and let Louise answer for me as she gave Bitsey a hug and assured Dad that "we girls" were indeed ready.

I was feeling a little apprehensive walking along toward the beach for I was reflecting on the disastrous events which our vacation had already provided. I was soon to find out that my apprehension was justified. Had I known what was in store for me I would have politely excused myself, returned to the cottage, climbed into the hide-a-bed, and let it fold up on me, staying there for the entire course of the Jamaican Holiday. But of course, pool old Ernie, always optimistic, always looking on the bright side of life, walked on, not knowing she was treading down Embarrassment Path.

We arrived at the beach just in time to hear a voice over the loudspeaker saying, "Ladies and gentlemen . . . and all you kids, too . . . welcome to Kickapoo Lake's Jamaican Holiday. We have quite an exciting, fun-filled day planned for you and hope you'll all stay right on until the end of the festivities."

Oh, Ernestine Cecelia Tubb stayed right on until the end of the festivities alright—right until the bitter end!

The voice went on, "And now, good people, we are going to start off our festival with our games. It's game time, everybody!"

"Goody, goody, games . . . prizes," squealed our little game girl.

"Our lifeguards," continued the voice, "have organized today's games and the winner will receive prizes appropriate for our Jamaican Holiday theme."

Louise and I exchanged dreamy looks at the mention of the lifeguards.

"The first event," continued the voice, "will be the three-legged sack race. So . . . come on, everybody, get a partner and head on down to the starting line. You'll see Nick down there handing out the burlap sacks."

"Come on, Ernie," said Louise, "let's see if we can win one of those Jamaican prizes."

"Sure thing," I returned, then added in a voice meant only for Louise's ears, "and get another chance to talk to Nick, too."

"Me too . . . me too!" hollered an excited Bitsey.

"Bitsey," said Dad, "you're going to be *my* partner."

"Oh, goody, goody . . . let's win, Daddy."

"Well . . . we'll sure try."

"Hi, Bitsey, quack, quack, quack!" It was Chester, of course, who had obviously undergone another transformation in the animal kingdom.

"Hi, quack, Chester."

"Quack, quack . . . are you going to run in the sack race?"

"Me and Daddy are gonna WIN!"

"Me, too," quacked the duck.

"No, Chester," I said, "it's a *sack* race, not a *quack* race."

He nodded his head, quacked once more, and waddled off toward the finish line.

"I'll follow the duck and wait for you over there." said Mom with a smile.

Louise and I hurried off to get our sack. I was busy trying to think of something witty and amusing to say to impress Nick, but the smile he gave us as he handed us our sack and his, "Good luck, girls," made my mind go completely blank. I guess Louise was affected the same way, for she didn't say anything to him either.

"Oh, Louise," I gushed as we walked to the starting line, "Did you see how Nick looked at us?"

"Oh, did I ever! You know, Ernie, I don't think he wished anyone else luck."

We were jarred from our trance-like state by a loud voice saying "Look who thinks they're going to win the sack race, Albert."

You can see how wrong Mom was with her prediction.

"Yeah . . . look who," was Albert's brilliant remark.

I gave Louise one of those wouldn't-you-know-it looks and said, "Well, Murphy, if your feet could go as fast as your

97

mouth, you'd definitely win."

Louise gave me a wink and Albert let go with a guffaw until the Mouth punched him on the shoulder and told him to shut his trap!

"Which leg do you want in the sack?" I asked Louise.

"How about you put your right one in the sack and I'll put my left one in."

"Sounds good to me."

"Maybe we should practice while we have time," suggested Louise, as we pulled up the sack.

"Gosh," I said, "it's hard enough just to walk like this, let alone run."

"I did this at our family reunion last summer," said Louise. "The trick is to hold on to one another's waist while one of us counts steps like this . . . step, two, step, two. Now on the word, step, we take a step with our legs in the sack and on two, we each take a step with the other leg."

"Let's try it," I said, "You count, Louise."

"Okay . . . here we go . . . step, two, step, two, step, two."

"Hey, that really works great," I said. "Geez, Louise, I sure am glad that you know what you're doing, otherwise, we might embarrass ourselves.

"Gosh, Ernie, maybe we *can* win one of those Jamaican prizes."

"Ernie, Wheez . . . look at me!"

We looked to one end of the starting line to see Dad and the little sack sweetheart. He was bent over holding the sack around himself and Bitsey. He looked back at us with a silly grin on his face and waved. Bitsey couldn't wave because both of her hands were clutching the sack. She was holding it so high that it was almost up to her neck.

"We won . . . we won!" she yelled.

I guess she thought the game was won by the pair who could get their sacks on the fastest, or hold them the highest, or some other dumb idea.

"We'd better get back to our starting place," I said.

"Ho, ho, ho . . . looked at the three-legged monster," said the colossal dumbbell.

"Ho, ho, ho," I shot back. "If it isn't Mutt and Jeff."

This broke Louise up as well as a few of the others lining up for the race. Actually, they did resemble Mutt and Jeff. Albert was a good foot shorter than old Megaphone-Mouth, and they really looked funny standing next to one another in a sack.

I was beginning to think that my clever retorts were a better strategy than my no-reaction routine in dealing with Murphy since his face turned a beautiful scarlet. I should have known better, though, for if there is one thing John can't stand, it's being laughed at. I should have guessed that it would only be a matter of time before the big lump would try to get even. Well, it didn't take him long.

Louise and I stood at the starting line waiting for Nick to begin the race.

"Move over, Tubby!" muttered Murphy as he and Albert pushed their way into line next to us.

"Isn't that just great," I asked myself. Louise gave me a knowing look.

"We're going to run all over you two," he threatened in a

low voice.

"Runners, take your marks," Nick called out.

"Murphy," I said, figuring I was already in for trouble, and it didn't matter anyhow, "why don't you give everybody a treat and put that sack over your head?"

"Yeah," said Louise, getting into the act. "Can't you see that 'Keep our beach beautiful sign over there?'"

Murphy flushed bright red again, opened his mouth and said, "Just you two wait, just you wait."

"Get ready," Nick continued. "Get set, GO!"

At the command of "Go!" Murphy shot out his big, dumb foot in front of mine in an effort to trip me. What he did in reality was to throw himself and Albert so completely off-balance that they fell over each other. Then, yes, you guessed it, they fell right into Louise and me. There the four of us were, sprawled out all over the starting line with all of the other racers leaving us in the dust.

"You big, stupid oaf!" I yelled as we all tried desperately to get untangled and back on our feet and to make a mad dash for the finish line.

"Albert . . . hurry up!"

"Well, you knocked me over," complained his whining partner.

Louise and I yanked up the sack and were off with her half shouting . . . step, two, step, two. Unfortunately our feet couldn't keep up with her shouts . . . we didn't get beyond that first step. You see, due to my hurry to get back into the race, and my unnerved condition what I did was to place both—I'll repeat that—BOTH of my legs into the sack. You can imagine the astonishment I experienced when I attempted to take that first step! You can imagine Louise's astonishment when, for the second time in so many seconds, I began falling again, pulling her down with me. Now that was bad enough, but it became even worse—it became the ultimate in embarrassment! You see, the dynamic duo of sack racers fell right into Mutt and Jeff who were still struggling to get back into their sack!

"Hey!" yelled a startled Mouth as he tumbled into Albert.

There we were, in one big, sandy heap. Legs and arms flying in every direction, all working desperately to get back up and into the race. We stopped when the sound of cheers at the other end of the beach reached us. The four of us looked up as if we were one . . . just in time to see Dad and Bitsey go streaking across the finish line!

CHAPTER TWELVE

The remainder of the afternoon consisted of a succession of lost races for Louise and me, and loud bangs, courtesy of Bitsey and her authentic Jamaican prize—a small steel drum.

Last year when we were studying a unit of the Caribbean our teacher, Ms. Fizz, had brought in one of these drums, along with a recording of a group she had heard while visiting Jamaica. Somehow the lovely music on the recording and the thumping bangs made by our amateur musician bore absolutely no resemblance to each other.

Since every game winner was awarded one of these steel drums, Kickapoo Lake resounded with an unharmonic medley of thumps, crashes, and bangs by the time dinner was served. Most of the "drummers" were children of Bitsey's age, and each darling little midget seemed to be competing for the "Nobody-else-can-beat-their-drum-this-loud" title.

"Louise," I said, in between the unrelenting thumps, bangs, and crashes, "if this is a sample of life in Jamaica, it should slide off the side of the earth. The side farthest from Pleasant Valley!"

She nodded her head in agreement, having long ago given up on trying to make herself heard over the "symphony."

The most marvelous thing about dinner, other than we were starving, was that the mighty midget band was put to rest while everyone got ready to eat. Tables were stacked high with food that had been prepared and brought to the beach in a van. All sorts of delicious and mouth-watering odors filled the air. We all lined up and piled our plates high wanting to sample everything . . . except for Bitsey, of course. Do you know what she wanted to eat? A peanut butter and jelly sandwich. Isn't that the limit? She never wants to try anything new. Mom put a few things on her plate and promised that after the feast she and Dad would take her back to the cottage for her . . . ugh . . . sandwich.

"Besides," said Mom, "I'm really beat. It's been a long day."

"Me too," added Dad, who was still a little sore from his adventure on the Water Whip. "Let's just spend a nice peaceful evening sitting on the porch. You girls can stay on for the E-N-T-E-R-T-A-I-N-M-E-N-T."

"What's that, Daddy?" asked the spelling whiz.

"Oh, that's for cleaning up the beach after dinner," said Dad with a straight face.

I looked at Louise and rolled my eyes, "Can you believe that?" I whispered.

We all wound up going back to the cottage after dinner because Louise and I wanted to change into our "special" outfits for the E-N-T-E-R-T-A-I-N-M-E-N-T. Mom and Dad collapsed into their lawn chairs as we went into the cottage to change. Bitsey rushed to get her Uncle Waddle's Barnyard game, minus the pig, to play with Dad. She seemed to have forgotten all about the peanut butter and jelly sandwich.

"What are you wearing, Louise?"

"My yellow and tan outfit. How about you, Ernie?"

"Oh, I like that one. You look really good in it," I answered. "I'm wearing my white and lavender one."

"Neat," responded Louise.

You may remember my special white and lavender outfit that went for a plunge off the dock. Dad managed to get it clean, but it had shrunk a little in the process.

"Well, we're on our way," I said as we came out the door.

"That's good . . . have fun," said Dad.

"Oh, Ernie," Mom eyed me critically, "do you think you should be wearing that outfit. It's awfully tight now."

"Oh, Mom," I groaned, "it's not *my* fault it got wet," and I glared in Bitsey's direction.

"Helen, let her go." said Dad, sticking up for me. "I think she looks great in it."

"Oh, alright," agreed Mom reluctantly, "But I still think it's too tight."

Acutally, I liked my outfit all the more since it shrunk. I was hoping that Nick would notice.

"Goodbye," Louise and I chorused.

"Bye," said Mom.

"Have a great time!" added Dad.

As we arrived at the beach, we could see a large crowd gathered around a band . . . and not an amateur steel band, thank goodness.

"Oh, gosh," said Louise, "it's the Things!"

"Are your sure?" I asked excitedly.

"I'd recognize *their* sound anywhere!"

You see, the Things was a local band. No . . . it was *the* local band. They play for all of the high school dances. Last year they played for the Junior High School dance to which all of the sixth graders were invited. All the girls in our class thought they were real dreamy. Of course, the dance was ruined when the big oaf, John Murphy, got out on the floor. He was the only boy on the dance floor and was pretending to be dancing. Actually he was hopping around bumping into the serious dancers—the girls—making them stumble and miss their steps.

The sound of quacking quickly brought me back to the present.

"Quack, quack, where's Bitsey?"

"She's back at the cottage, Chester," I explained.

"Quack, quack, why is she there?"

"Because she wants to be there," I continued tolerantly.

"Quack, quack, why does she want to be there?"

I snapped, "She's tired," having lost patience with being cross-examined by a duck.

"It's too bad," I said to Louise, "that they didn't gather up all of the ducks around here and roast them for dinner."

Louise giggled, "That would have solved your problem."

"Quack, quack, why is she tired?"

"Goodbye Chester," I said.

"Goodbye, quack, quack," he continued to stand there staring at me.

"Chester, I said 'goodbye.'"

"Goodbye, quack, quack." He didn't budge an inch.

I was beginning to wonder if he had decided that he was now a parrot. I gave the duck one more try.

"Chester," I told him, "they are about to give out the Big Dumb Duck award. You're sure to win it, but you better get right over to the bandstand to claim it."

"Goodbye, quack, quack," said Chester as he broke into a fast waddle . . . in the opposite direction from the bandstand.

"Boy . . . he really is something else," said Louise.

"He sure is," I agreed. "His parents should take him to a doctor for tests, but I bet they're afraid they'd lock him up in a padded cell."

Louise laughed, "Or maybe they're afraid they wouldn't."

Just then the Things finished their number and Joe, one of the lifeguards, went up to the microphone.

"Now for something very special for all you good folks. Since this is Jamaican night, we are going to have a contest doing something that is very popular in Jamaica. It is called the LIMBO!"

Several people in the crowd let out cheers. Louise and I pushed our way closer to the bandstand so we could see what a limbo was.

"You can see that Nick and Bruce are holding a long pole between them," Joe continued. "Right now, it's pretty high above the ground, but as the band plays, it will slowly be lowered. Each of you who enters the contest must keep on dancing under the pole as it gets lower and lower. Now here's the tricky part. You can only go under the pole by bending

106

backwards . . . yes, backwards. Tracy will show you how."

Tracy was one of the lifeguards and as the band began to play, she danced under the pole several times as Nick and Bruce lowered it.

"Get the idea, folks?" asked Joe. "It's time for the contest to begin. The lucky person to wiggle under the pole at its lowest level is the winner. And, the prize is *not* another steel drum!"

His announcement brought applause, laughs and one or two cheers from the crowd.

"Come on, Ernie," said Louise and she hurried to get into line.

"Okay," I said, following her like a lamb being led to slaughter. "It looks easy enough."

"Hey, Albert, how do you suppose a great big Tubb can ever get itself under that little pole?"

"Big Tubb . . . yeah," came the sidekick's clever response.

After the great sack race calamity, I had decided to revert to my no-reaction-to-the Mouth strategy to deal with Murphy. Louise took her cue from me and ignored them too.

The line began to move as everyone went under the pole without any trouble at all.

"Gosh, that *was* easy," I told Louise.

"It sure was," she agreed, as we watched the pole being lowered.

We passed under it several more times without any problems. That's when Joe said, "Well, it seems that you all have the knack for doing the limbo."

Louise and I gave one another pleased looks, getting more

hopeful about winning.

"But now," he continued, "comes the fun. Bruce and Nick, stop being so nice, I want to see that pole lowered at a faster rate. And you Things, let's have some really *fast* music to help determine who the *real* limbo experts are."

"Boy, is this ever getting exciting," exclaimed Louise, as she began bending under the pole.

I was next and boy, did I ever have to bend way over backwards. My new shorts and top really pulled on me when I did this. I knew now Mom was right . . . they were too tight and that was going to handicap me in this contest. As I was just under pole, I heard, "Look out, everyone, here comes Tubby the Whale!"

I felt my face go red and not just from the strain of the limbo. Stupid dumb-head . . . he would have to start in right in front of Nick.

"Just ignore him," whispered Louise as I caught up with her in line. We could see the two nitwits laughing and whispering together.

"Now what do you suppose they're up to?" I asked Louise.

"Up to no good, you can bet on that," she answered.

"Yes," I agreed. "They're probably thinking up dumb things to call us."

Most of the adults in the limbo line hadn't made it under the pole the last time, so the line was suddenly much shorter. Before we knew it, it was Louise's turn again.

"Oh, no . . . look how low it is now," she shuddered. "Wish me luck!"

"Good luck, and just ignore any remarks from the two birdbrains," I said loudly as she began to slide under the pole.

She was almost through when the mouth yelled, "Son of Blubber squeezes through!"

I saw Louise stiffen a little and I turned and glared at the pair of laughing hyenas.

"You're next, Ernie," hollered Nick. I almost fainted dead away, right there on the spot. *Nick* knew my name! Suddenly my vacation was wonderful. All of the horrendous things that had happened faded away to nothing . . . all previous disasters vanished from my memory. *Nick* knew my name! Well, let me tell you that Nick, and for that matter, everyone else in the crowd would *never forget* the name of Ernestine Cecelia Tubb because of what happened next.

"Good luck!" yelled Louise as I began my struggle to get under the pole. Over I leaned . . . farther and farther.

"There goes Blubber-Britches," Nitwit yelled. It didn't matter, I was expecting it and besides . . . *Nick* knew my name.

I was almost under the pole when the utmost disaster took place. Oh, you say, you knocked over the pole? No, I did not knock over the pole. Well, you say, you ran into Nick! No, I did not run into Nick. Of course, you say, you fell down! No, I did not fall down. Come on, your really have to think . . . disaster! Let me describe disaster to you. You see, as Ernestine Cecelia Tubb leaned over as far as she could, getting dizzy from a lack of oxygen . . . her shorts split right up the side! SPLIT! And naturally, the split was on the side next to where Nick was standing. I wanted to die! I thought I would. I raised up as fast as I could, knocking the pole out of Nick and Bruce's hands.

"Woo . . . woo . . . woo!" guffawed the Big-Babble-Mouth. "Now that's what I call a real SIDE SHOW!

Nick, being the gentleman he is, quickly found a beach towel which Louise helped me wrap myself in. Needless to say, we headed straight for the cottage. As we started up the cottage steps, Dad spotted us and called, "Hi, girls, did you have as much fun as you thought you would?"

"My, my," I thought to myself, "What a perfect ending to such a perfect day!"

CHAPTER THIRTEEN

"Oh, Pete, I just don't think that it's really a very good idea," Mom was shaking her head as she and Dad came out of the cottage after washing the breakfast dishes. They had made a deal with Louise and me that they'd do the dishes while we took Bitsey outside with us. Personally, I think *they* got the better deal.

"Oh, come on, Helen," Dad argued. "You can at least try it. You don't know what you're missing."

"I think it's more the case that *you* don't know what you're getting us into," Mom replied.

Then she looked at Dad, smiled, and said, "I can't stand that pleading look on you face! Are you sure you really want to do it?"

"I'm absolutely positive about this, Helen," he nodded his head.

"Well, alright . . . but I'm absolutely positive it's going to be the most *boring* afternoon I've ever spent."

Well, as I've told you before, when Mom is wrong, she's really wrong . . . and today was no exception.

111

"Now, Helen, it's our last day here at Kickapoo Lake and you haven't even been out in the boat once. I've gone out fishing several times and had such fun. I just want to share the fun of fishing with everyone. And as for your being bored . . . nonsense. You'll feel like a new woman after being out on the lake with all of us together."

"Fishing," I thought. "In the Queen Elizabeth! All five of us, make that five and a half, her highness couldn't go without Claudie. My, my, that certainly does sound like fun!"

"Girls," announced Dad, "since this is our last full day at the lake, I have a very special treat in store for all of us."

He must have thought we had suddenly gone deaf. We had been standing right there all the time he and Mom were arguing.

"Candy . . . candy . . . candy!" chirped the little sweet tooth girl.

"Oh, no, honey," beamed Dad. "This is something you're going to enjoy a lot more than candy."

The chocolate princess was really puzzled by Dad's response since she just can't imagine *anything* being better than candy.

"Today," Dad continued, as if his proclamation was being televised, "is the day that the Tubb family . . . Louise, I consider you a part of our family . . ."

"Thank you, Mr. Tubb," smiled Louise.

". . . Yes, today the Tubb family is going to have a great time because we are all going to go fishing together."

"I wanna fishie."

Dad was really rolling by now, so he ignored the I-wanna girl.

"There is no better way to bring a family together than in the warm and friendly closeness one feels while fishing together. Yes . . ."

"Oh, for heaven's sakes," interrupted Mom. "Enough is enough!"

"But, Helen, I just want to make sure that everyone appreciates what we're about to do together."

If he had known then, how "what we're about to do together" would turn out he would have defintely used a word other than "appreciate!"

"Pete . . . I'm sure we all will, without any more speech-making on your part."

Louise and I grinned at each other. We both had witnessed how Dad can get all wrapped up in one of his projects. We had only to think of last November and a certain old-fashioned Thanksgiving to remind us.

"I wanna fishie, Daddy," went the broken record.

"Well, honey, I'm sure you'll get a fish today."

Bitsey just beamed at his statement. I imagine that she planned on dressing it up and having tea with it. Mom went back into the cottage to prepare a lunch basket to take with us while Dad went out to the Queen Elizabeth to get the fishing gear in order . . . oh, yes, and to bail a little, too.

"Claudie wanna fishie, too,"

"Boy, wouldn't Claude just *love* a fishie," I said, giving Louise the eye.

"Claudie and fishie play Waddie Widdle's Yarn with Bitsey."

Louise looked at me questioningly as if she was wondering how to explain what happens to fishies once they get caught.

I just shrugged and said, "We'll let Dad explain when, I mean, if, the time comes when we need to."

It wasn't long before the Tubb family had all boarded their rather unseaworthy craft. The anchor was lifted and, in Dad's own words, we were off on the Tubb family's great fishing expedition.

"Giddy-up."

"Here we go again," I told Louise, as we took turns bailing. Just then, I had a terrible thought.

"Dad?"

"Yes, Ernie," he grunted since he was doing the rowing.

"Dad . . . you don't fish in the lilypads, do you?"

"No," he laughed, "don't worry, Ernie, we won't go near the lilypads."

"Claudie wanna litty."

I could hear Mom trying to distract Bitsey's mind from the litty. Louise and I were sitting on the back seat, Mom on the front middle seat, and her highness perched on her throne in front, clutching Claudie tightly. Of course, Mom and Dad had absolutely forbidden Bitsey to bring Claudie on our fishing adventure. And, of course, after throwing one of her famous, furious fits, Bitsey was allowed to bring the unwilling fisherman. It wasn't long until our small band arrived at THE SPOT.

"This is it," said a huffing and puffing Dad as he pulled in the oars. "This is where the fish just beg to be caught. Yes, this is the spot alright."

"Claudie," explained tongue-twister Tillie, "this is the pot. This is where the fishies sit up and beg in the pot."

"Ernie," ordered the ship's commander, "throw out the anchor so we don't drift away from this great old fishing hole."

"Okay," I responded, picking up the heavy metal anchor and slowly lowering it over the back of the boat.

"Claudie," continued the interpreter, "we gotta be careful . . . there's a hole in the fishing pot."

Mom, Dad, and Louise began laughing, but not me. After all, when one has to deal with Bitsey's mixed-up messages day after day, one tends to lose one's sense of humor about them.

As soon as the anchor was secure, Dad began his great "How to Fish" lecture. Since none of us had been fishing, we all listened intently. Believe it or not, even Bitsey was attentive. She obviously was taking her responsibility to repeat the instructions to her Claudie seriously.

"Now it's really quite simple. Each of us will have a pole," he smiled as he passed them out to everybody. "Bitsey, I'll hold your pole until I'm finished explaining, then help you."

"Sank you, Daddy," she responded as if she had just been handed a glowing compliment.

"Now you must be very careful of the hook," continued Dad. "I have already placed the latex worms on them for you."

I was very relieved to discover we would not be using live bait. By Louise's expression, she felt the same way.

"It's very important that we keep our poles as far apart as possible . . . we don't want to get the lines tangled. That could be a problem."

Considering the size of the Queen Elizabeth I figured that would be quite a stunt.

"Now, simply lower your lines into the water until your bobbers are floating. Then when you see your bobber being pulled into the water, simply jerk up on the pole. Maybe, just maybe, you have caught your first fish!"

"Oh, goody, goody, goody. Claudie and Bitsey caught a fishie."

"Brother," I thought as Mom, Louise and I placed our lines into the water. Dad moved forward past Mom to help her highness. Soon we were all busy with the absorbing task of watching our bobbers float on the water.

"My," I said to myself, "Isn't this exciting! I'm so excited I'm almost asleep."

Little did I know just how exciting it would soon be aboard our little vessel.

Whether or not my dear little sister actually *saw* her bobber being pulled under the water is really unimportant. What is important is her reaction.

"Aaaaaaahhhhhhhh!" she screamed, throwing the fishing pole straight up into the air. This scared her Claude so badly that he began racing around the boat. Dad made a mad scramble to catch the flying fishing pole before it went the way of Bitsey's piggy . . . lost forever in the deep blue. Poor Dad was in such a hurry to reach the pole that he forgot to watch where he was going and was tripped, either by Mom's seat, or by a terrified cat. He crashed down into the bottom of the boat with a loud, splintering noise.

"Oh, no," yelled Mom, for the water was beginning to leak into the boat at an alarming speed.

"Ernie, Louise!" she kept on yelling. "Get the anchor . . . and bail as fast as you can!"

116

She fitted the oars into the oarlocks and began rowing while my somewhat dazed father pulled himself up to a sitting position and gropingly worked his way to the oars. Mom slid over and they each rowed furiously with one oar. The water kept coming in faster and faster. Louise and I were bailing at a rapid rate, but we simply couldn't get ahead of the incoming water.

"Bail faster," Mom shouted.

"Giddy-up," screamed an excited Bitsey. She was again clutching her retrieved Claude.

I think that the Tubb family must have set an all-world's record for rowing a sinking boat halfway across Kickapoo Lake. But we made it . . . almost. We couldn't have been more than two feet from our dock when the Queen simply gave up and ever so slowly sank the three feet to the bottom, with the entire, exhausted Tubb family still on board.

Dad grabbed Bitsey and Claude while the rest of us attempted to save what little we could.

"Gosh," I thought, "Dad was certainly right, fishing really does bring a family together."

CHAPTER FOURTEEN

Nick and I were dancing to the music of the Things and I felt like I'd died and gone to heaven, when suddenly the tune we were dancing to turned into "Mary Had a Little Lamb." I found this to be very confusing . . . but only for a moment. That was the moment it took me to fully wake up and find myself next to Louise in our hide-a-bed, and not in Nick's arms at all! The strains of "Mary Had a Little Lamb" still echoed in my ears and no wonder . . . that was the song Bitsey chose to honor us with on her regular morning serenade. Our little song stylist had, of course, adapted the words to suit herself. It was this song that brought me out of my lovely dream world, back into harsh reality.

> Bitsey had a little Claudie,
> Little Claudie, little Claudie
> Bitsey swam with Little Claudie
> All over Kipoowee Lake!

My little sister seems to have the unique talent of making each of her songs, as unlikely as it seems, more monotonous than the preceding ones. Over and over and over again her song went on, with her unmelodic voice rising in volume with each repetition. I put the pillow over my head in hopes of stemming the assault on my ears, but it was no use. That piercing voice of hers would probably penetrate a solid lead wall.

"Oh, well," I thought, giving Louise a nudge, "might as well get up."

She was already awake, of course. It was impossible for anyone to sleep once the Kickapoo Lake jaybird began screeching.

"Morning, Ernie," said a bleary-eyed Louise.

"Morning," I responded.

"Good morning, everybody," called Dad, as he came in through the back door. "Mom and I are having breakfast down by the lake. Come on, you sleepyheads, get out of bed and join us. It's a glorious morning."

I felt his enthusiasm was a little overdone considering how early it was, and the rude manner in which Louise and I had been awakened. Louise and I managed to mumble, "Okay, Mr. Tubb," and "Right, Dad," but the wake-up girl tumbled out of bed and streaked past Dad out the back door, dragging a half-asleep Claude with her.

"After breakfast," Dad continued, "we're going to have to begin picking up the cottage and packing for home."

"Oh, gosh," said Louise, "that's really sad. I've had such a great time that I don't want our vacation ever to end."

"I'm glad to hear that, Louise," smiled Dad. "We're just so happy that you came with us. Now hurry, you two, get out there before your breakfast disappears into Claude."

"You're right, Louise," I said, as the door banged shut after

Dad. "This *is* kind of sad, isn't it?"

I was rather surprised to hear myself saying that, let alone feeling that way.

"Oh, Ernie . . . haven't we had fun!" laughed Louise.

"Yeah . . . I guess we really have," I agreed, as we climbed into our clothes. "But I'll have to admit that at times I would have preferred a cold, damp dungeon to being here. You know . . . the time Claude and I went diving for lilypads!"

We both laughed at the memory of that incident, something I would have never imagined possible at the time.

"Geez, Louise," I said as we walked to our waiting breakfast, "some of the things that seemed so awful when they happen-ed seem kind of funny now."

"Good morning, girls," waved Mom as we approached.

"Morning," we both chorused.

"We have juice, milk, and breakfast rolls," announced Dad. "Help yourselves."

Bitsey and Claude were already sharing one of the princess's favorite kinds of breakfast rolls . . . a creamy butter nut delight.

"Claudie want some more cutty light?" asked our little linguist.

"Mom," I asked, with a mouth half-full of a "cutty light," "will Louise and I have time this morning to take one last swim?"

"Oh, I think so," she answered, "on one condition."

Well, it didn't take a genius to figure out that one condi-tion, so I simply pleaded, "You mean we *have* to take her?"

"Ernie," responded Mom, "it would be a big help to your

father and me as we are doing the packing."

"Oh, but Mom, it's our very last swim." I gave her an imploring look, hoping that I might play on her sympathy so Louise and I could go off alone.

But then Dad said in that tone I've never questioned, "Ernestine!"

So, after breakfast, the three of us . . . at least, we didn't have to take Claude along . . . grabbed our towels and headed for our last swim at Kickapoo Lake. And, incidently, our last look at the beautiful Nick.

For the first time in a week Ernestine Cecelia Tubb was now looking out of two normal eyes. Yes, Dad was right . . . my black eye had taken a week to disappear.

"Oh, Ernie," said Louise, as we neared the Water Whip. "Do you remember our adventure there?"

"Boy, do I remember! Louise, I won't forget it in a million years. Unfortunately, neither will anyone else! Particularly that Big-mouth-who-tells-everybody-he-knows John Murphy. Why, next year at junior high I bet he tells all the kids. Boy, what a wonderful way to start out at a new school!"

"Oh, Ernie, I bet he forgets all about it by this fall."

"Louise . . . he never forgets anything! You can be sure he'll babble on about the Water Whip . . . and he won't waste any time describing what he called my 'side-show' during the limbo either."

"Well, at least he doesn't know anything about the sinking of the Queen Elizabeth," Louise said in a comforting voice, attempting to make me feel better.

"No . . . I guess I should be thankful for small favors," I

said as we placed our towels on the sand for the last time.

"Bitsey gonna make a sandy house," declared the little construction engineer as she carried her pail and shovel toward the water.

"Well," smiled Louise, "shall we take our last swim?"

"Stop it . . . you're making me feel so sad," I told her.

"If you really want to feel sad . . . think about taking your last look at Nick!"

"Geez, Louise . . . that doesn't make me feel sad . . . that makes me feel terribly depressed!" We both laughed as we waded into the water.

We swam for as long as we thought we dared, then decided to go back to the cottage to help finish the packing . . . if it wasn't all done by now.

"Come on, Bitsey," I hollered as Louise and I picked up our towels and began drying off. "Mom and Dad are probably waiting for us to come back and help pack."

"Does that mean you're leaving so soon?"

Louise and I whirled around to see Nick standing behind us. I could just feel my face flushing to a bright red, and I heard a slight sigh come from Louise.

"Ah . . . yes," came my brilliant reply. I felt like Albert.

"That's too bad," he said. "You certainly livened things up around here this past week."

"Oh, Nick," I thought, "you don't know the half of it . . . thank goodness."

Louise and I just stood there like the two village idiots, unable to say one word between us.

"Well . . . I guess this is goodbye then," he said. "Maybe

I'll see you in the fall. You're starting junior high, aren't you?"

I did manage a nod while Louise squeaked a "yes."

"Well, if you come to any of the senior high football games you'll probably see me. Look for the quarterback."

I found my voice at last to the marvelous extent of being able to stammer, "Oh, great . . . we'll be there."

"Good," he said, turning to leave.

"Bye," Louise and I told him together.

"Goodbye," he returned.

"Bye, bye, Mr. Bootiful," came the piercing voice.

Louise and I each grabbed hold of one of the midget's hands and started her on a running walk before she could say anything else.

"Goodbye, honey," laughed Nick as we left the beach.

"We've just about finished packing," said Dad, putting things in the trunk of the car. "By the time you girls change into your clothes we should be all ready to start back to Pleasant Valley."

"Wheez, Wheez, I wanna play the car game!"

"Sure, Bitsey," agreed Louise. "You'll have to wait until we're on the road, though."

Bitsey's request brought back the wonderful memories of our trip to the lake just one week ago. I quickly surveyed the sky for rain clouds and was terribly relieved to see it was a bright clear blue.

There *was* a dark, cloudy sky above, as I would soon learn, hanging over the Cecil T. Squat Junior High School, just waiting to open up on me as I walked through the doors!